Reb slid the pistol into his belt and walked to the door, his jaw tight.

Bert was standing in the wide doorway, telling the crowd to bust it up and go on home. But when they saw Reb, the chatter increased. Bert turned "Damnit, Reb, stay back in there!"

But Reb pushed past him, looking for Curly. And the crowd suddenly parted, getting out of the line of fire; men scrambled, staring at him.

Curly stood in the middle of the street, scowling, thumbs hooked in his cartridge belt.

Reb halted, looked at Curly, and smiled.

And Curly went for his gun.

Also by Arthur Moore
Published by Fawcett Books:

THE KID FROM RINCON
TRAIL OF THE GATLINGS
THE STEEL BOX
DEAD OR ALIVE
MURDER ROAD
ACROSS THE RED RIVER
THE HUNTERS
THE OUTLAWS

REBEL

Arthur Moore

FAWCETT GOLD MEDAL • NEW YORK

A Fawcett Gold Medal Book
Published by Ballantine Books
Copyright © 1992 by Arthur Moore

Library of Congress Catalog Card Number: 91-93155

ISBN 0-449-14780-0

Manufactured in the United States of America

First Edition: April 1992

1

He was the only son of Todd and Leona Wiley, a big, raw-boned lad who moved like a cat. His name was Rydal, after a grandfather, but everyone called him Rebel.

He had eyes that were blue or gray, depending on the light; his hair was brown and straight, cut short by his father's razor. There had been a barber in Rustin, but he had decamped after a fracas in the Senate Saloon at the edge of town. The barber had beaten up one of the crib girls—or so the saloon owner had said. He had fired two shots at the barber—one had smashed a watchmaker's sign, the other had missed the agile scissors wielder, who had then taken the next stage.

Rebel's uncle Isham, brother of his mother, lived only a short distance from the Wiley house on Tilford Street, one of the two streets in the town, the other being Main Street, of course, that some called Front Street. There were other byways, but none that could be dignified by the name of street.

Rustin was a tiny dot on the prairie, its only reason for being that it was set down plunk on the crossroads trails that had been there since the devil had invented cyclones. And now it was a stage stop on the way to the big towns farther east, like Berham and Machen. Machen was the county seat and boasted a population of nearly two thousand souls.

Rebel worked for his father when there was no one to teach in the single-room schoolhouse. There hadn't been a teacher in two years and anyhow, at sixteen years old, he was getting too big for that sort of thing.

His father ran a few cows, maybe thirty, and did some farming. He had a hundred and sixty acres of prairie sod on which he'd built a good solid shack with a puncheon floor and a tarpaper roof. There was an outhouse down the slope a hundred feet or so. The house and outbuilding stood a mile from town and Reb and his father stayed there now and then, sleeping on the two iron cots in the shack. They mended fences and chopped weeds, among the host of other chores.

Todd Wiley had plans for a larger structure—a barn—but the plans had been put aside for the time being because of cost. The barn and some sheds would probably price out at near three hundred dollars. Wood would have to be hauled from Berham, no simple task. Todd had made the trip to Machen two years past, to talk to Hiram Biggs, the banker. Biggs was willing to advance the three hundred, but Todd had been leery of going that far into debt, as he talked it over with Leona, and so the matter rested.

But Todd still talked about increasing the herd. People were buying cattle down south on the Arkansas, at towns like Dodge, and it made him itchy, he said, to think of all the money they were missing out on.

Rebel listened to the talk, very interested. Uncle Isham came 'round at least once a week to sit on the porch and drink lemonade and argue with Todd. Isham said he had a few dollars saved, his wife was gone now, and he was alone and eager to go into the cow business with Todd. Between them they could sign the loan papers and go looking to buy critters . . . if Todd would agree.

But his father didn't jump at it. Todd was a cautious man and counted his pennies. Damn cautious, Reb thought.

It sounded good. Reb would give an arm to see Dodge, or one of the cow towns. Just see it, listen to it. Hell, he could walk through Rustin, from one end to the other, in something like four minutes.

Twice a week he went down to the stage station and watched the Concord and six come in. On Wednesdays it

came from the west, on Saturdays from the east. Sometimes
it held six or seven passengers. Occasionally only one or two.
Reb would lean against the wall and stare at them, wondering
where they had come from and what they had done and where
they were going. . . . None ever got off and stayed in Rustin.

How he longed to board the stage and go—somewhere!

Once in a while one or two painted women would get
down, looking about curiously. They always went into the
waiting room and the small restaurant. He saw one of them
light a thin brown cigar one day and it shocked him. He could
not get it out of his mind for the longest time. . . .

He had only one real friend in the town, Lem Cotter. Lem
was his age, a bookworm. He read the weekly that came
from Machen, from front to back; he borrowed books and
had his nose in them constantly. He had even read the Bible
twice, he said.

And Lem knew about painted women . . . from his books.
"They're whores," he said. "They probably come from
some place in the East, looking to work in a dance hall."

Rebel had seen whores before, at the Senate Saloon. Only
those women looked much older than the ones he'd seen on
the stages.

But women did not hold his attention. Guns did. His father
owned a sixteen-gauge shotgun of Swiss manufacture. Todd
had bought it years before Reb had been born and used it
hunting quail and rabbits. He and Isham had been going
hunting for decades, when the weather permitted.

When Reb had been eight or nine, he had tagged along
and had been allowed to shoot the shotgun. Isham had a
small carbine, .36-caliber, and a big .44 revolver made by
Colt. Reb eyed the pistol Isham wore in his belt, wishing he
could get his hands on it.

Todd and Isham were both of a size, big broad men, Isham
with a drooping mustache, Todd clean-shaven. They had large
callused hands, very powerful, and were slow to change
opinions. They rode horses out on the open prairie where
Todd shot a few quail and a couple of rabbits.

The first time Reb fired the shotgun he brought down a low-flying quail.

Isham remarked that it was beginner's luck.

"You told me to lead the bird," Reb said.

"Yes—you did it just right," his father said, taking the gun. "Now go get your bird."

They saw no more quail that day, and on the way back they halted and got down. Isham set up a row of small stones on larger ones. He paced off fifty yards and handed the carbine to the boy. "Let's see you knock off those stones."

"It's too damn far for him," Todd objected.

Reb hefted the short rifle for the first time and looked at the sights. The rear sight was slightly bent. The front sight had been repaired; a long time ago someone had welded a bit of coin to make the sight.

Isham said, "It pulls a mite to the left."

Reb looked at him. "How big is a mite?"

Isham laughed. "Well, it's guesswork. It depends on the distance. Fire a shot, and you'll see."

Reb looked down the sights. A mite to the left? He aimed at the edge of the rock and squeezed the trigger. At the shot the rock disappeared and both men yelled.

"Try the next one," Isham urged.

Rebel knocked off every small rock, one after the other, firing quickly.

Todd whistled. "That's beginner's luck?"

"The kid's got an eye for it," Isham admitted. He walked out and set up six more rocks, this time at twenty-five paces. When he returned to them, he pulled the Colt revolver. "Let's see what you can do with this."

Reb's eyes lighted up as he received the heavy gun. He handled it reverently. Isham showed him how to open the loading gate.

"It's got six beans in it. This one shoots straight and the trigger is lighter'n the carbine. I mean it don't take much to set 'er off." As Reb pointed the pistol Isham said, "Let your thumb rest easy when you squeeze. . . ."

Holding the gun with both hands, Reb aimed at the rock

and took up the trigger slack. It fired before he thought it would, but the rock disappeared.

Both men yelled again and Todd pounded his son on the back. "He's a damn natural!"

"Let's see if it was luck," Isham said. "Hit the next rock."

Reb pointed the big pistol and pulled the hammer back. This time he was ready. He squeezed, and when the gun fired, the second rock disappeared. He yanked back the hammer and fired at the third. It went, too. He heard Isham say, "Jesus Christ!"

He knocked all six rocks off their perches and grinned at his elders. They were staring at him as if he had suddenly turned bright blue.

"I never saw nothing like it," Isham said in a hollow voice. He stood over Reb, glowering. "You been out here practicin', boy? You said you never fired a pistol before!"

"I never did," Reb said, shaking his head. He handed the revolver back.

"Nobody's gonna believe it," Isham said, sighing.

Todd grunted. He slid an arm about his son's shoulders. "He's just a natural-born shot, that's all. Got an eye like a goddamn eagle!"

2

He had always been able to outdo other boys. He could run faster, jump farther, and box better. Lem would never get into a contest with him. It was no use, Lem said.

There were five other boys near their age in the town. Three were a little older, but none could come close to besting Reb at any sport. The oldest was stronger, but Reb was more agile, and when they boxed, the older boy was easily outpointed.

It was his coordination, people who watched him agreed. One man who boxed in the saloon for money said, "That kid's got more by-Jesus talent than I ever seen."

He was a natural-born athlete, Lem told everyone. Some people are lucky that way. Some are born with red hair and some with six toes, but Reb was quick and sure at everything.

Some folks suggested to Todd that in a few years his son might make a pile of money by traveling from one saloon to another challenging the local toughs to bare-knuckled fights.

"You mean those pass-the-hat fights?"

"Sure. Why not?"

Todd growled. "No son of mine is gonna sink that low."

"Well, if you don't want him to fight, then he could footrace. He could travel from one country fair to the next. What's wrong with footracin'?"

"It's not a man's job."

Reb was not impressed with any of the suggestions—though the idea of joining a circus as a trickshot artist appealed to him. He thought about it quite a bit as he lay in

6

bed staring into the dark. Travel from one place to another! Of course he knew the circus laid up in the winter . . . but the idea of travel was fascinating.

However, when he talked to Lem Cotter about it, Lem poured cold water on the subject. "Those small circuses are composed of crooks and other shady characters. It sounds good, but it's a hard life and they're usually one jump ahead of the law."

"How do you know all that?"

Lem shrugged. "It's in the newspapers all the time."

"Then what would you do if you were me?"

"God knows," Lem said, staring at him thoughtfully. "I might try for West Point or Annapolis."

Reb was astonished. "Be a soldier?" Fort Hendley was close by and there were blue-clad soldiers in the town every day, usually in the saloons, now and then lying in the street at night, drunk and howling.

"I'm talking about becoming an officer. The government will pay for your education—if you can get an appointment."

Reb shook his head. "I don't think I'd like it."

"And there's a pension at the end of it."

"Yes, but it's not for me."

What was for him?

It was time he was deciding. He had little desire to farm or herd cattle. What did he want? He rather thought his father expected him to join in the long-talked-about cow business with Isham.

How in the world could he avoid it? Probably he would have to go along with them and travel with a herd to Dodge or one of the other cow towns. At least it would be *some* travel. Maybe something would turn up. . . .

But not what he hoped or expected. Walking through town one evening, he met two soldiers.

Thinking about it afterward, he was not sure how the fracas started. He had not been paying them any attention. There were always off-duty troopers about. He was aware that one of them apparently put his foot out and tripped him. He could not be sure if it was not an accident. At first.

He found himself on his back in the middle of the dusty street, and he swore in annoyance. One of the two soldiers, a tall, skinny one, growled that no goddamn kid was gonna swear at him, and he lashed out with his boot. It partially connected as Reb rolled away. The second soldier, more stocky and muscled, was on him like a tiger, slamming blows into him as Reb tried to get up.

There was a ringing in his ears and he felt himself pummeled. The two men were swearing and kicking him—he felt pain in a dozen places. They crushed him against a wall and he saw white exploding lights as he fell, one hand before his face.

Dimly he heard someone shout his name and he blinked, trying to clear his head, ducking away from blows at the same time.

The voice yelled, ''Here, catch, Reb!''

In the next moment a pistol thudded into his stomach.

Reb grabbed it. The hammer came back and he fired at the closest bluecoat, aiming at the man's legs. He heard a scream as he fired at the second man and saw him spin away, arms flailing.

Only then was he conscious of a crowd of men around him, all yelling and shouting. . . . Reb got to his feet, leaning against the building, gasping for breath. The two soldiers were on the ground, one motionless, the other still moaning, holding his leg.

He looked at the pistol, wondering who had tossed it to him. It was a .38 Smith & Wesson. It had certainly evened the odds in a hurry.

The town constable, Henry Jorganson, appeared quickly, having heard the shots. He sent a man for the doc, looked at Reb with the gun, and began to ask questions.

The revolver belonged to Albe Newlan, the general-store owner. He took it back, saying he could not bear to see two big bullies beating up on a boy. The crowd agreed with him;

most said they thought the two men were about to kill Reb when Albe tossed the gun to him.

Albe pulled Reb into the store and put some stinging stuff on his wounds. He was badly cut about the face. Albe thought probably one of the men or both had worn heavy rings.

Jorganson came in after a bit to say the two soldiers had been taken away in a wagon. It was his opinion that one of them would never walk again without a cane. "You shot his goddamn kneecap off, Reb. Where was you aiming?"

"At his legs."

"You shoulda shot both of 'em in the damn gizzard. They was looking for trouble." He slapped Albe on the back. "Good thing you had that pistol handy. Saved the kid's bacon." He went out, slamming the door.

It was his first real, serious fight and the shakes set in after it was over. Lordy, he could have killed those two! But if Albe hadn't tossed him the Smith, they might have killed him.

He included Albe in his prayers that night.

In two weeks a hearing was held. It was not a trial. Two lawyers came from the county seat. One was a florid, be-whiskered man, very pompous and stiff. His name was Judson Locke and he presided over the hearing. The other lawyer was skinny as a rail, with a hawk face and hands too big for his arms. He conferred with several officers from the fort.

The proceedings took only a short time. Apparently half the town had seen the fight and all were willing to testify that the two soldiers had accosted Reb, who had merely defended himself.

One of the two soldiers was still in the hospital. He had been taken to Berham and, according to an officer from the fort, would never walk again without crutches. . . . The second man was in the room glaring at Reb. When he was called, he declared that Reb had called him names and he had merely cuffed the boy.

A half-dozen citizens jumped up to protest the lie. Mr. Locke had to use his gavel, and when order was restored, he proclaimed the hearing at an end. Rebel was free to go. There was no evidence for a trial. Locke did not look happy at this ruling, but it was evident he had no choice.

The man, still in bandages, was hustled out of the room by other soldiers, all scowling at Reb. The hurt man was called John Willet. Reb made a note of it.

The incident and the hearing provided the little town with conversation and gossip for weeks. Soldiers who pressed into the saloons talked loudly about the affair and the uppity kid who had shot two of their number and gotten away without punishment. A few threatened that their buddy Willet would get even one way or another.

According to the weekly, the man in the hospital in Berham was discharged from the army, which ruled that his wounds were caused by his own mischief. He was therefore out on his own, with only one leg.

John Willet was not seen in Rustin for a month.

Of course Reb received a mass of advice, most of which consisted of him making himself scarce when Willet appeared. Even Lem thought it might be what he called the better part of valor.

"He's a man straight out of the gutter," he told Reb. "He'll kill you if he can."

"I won't spend my life dodging him."

"Well, you might not be lucky enough to have Albe throw you a pistol next time."

Reb knew there was a lot of truth in that. The chances of Albe repeating the act were not great. But it sparked an idea in his mind. He went to the general store and hung around until there were no customers in the place.

Albe said, "What can I do f'you, Reb?"

Reb came directly to the point. "Will you sell me your pistol?"

Albe looked at him with no surprise. "Willet?"

"Yes."

"I didn't think you'd run away."

"I can't."

Albe nodded. "All right. It's worth five'r ten dollars. Give it to you for five. You got any money at all?"

"I can get it." Uncle Isham would sure loan him five.

Albe pursed his lips. "You can work if off here if you want. There's plenty to do."

Reb agreed quickly. They decided he would work in the store an hour or two each day for a month, and the Smith & Wesson would become his. In the meantime he took possession of it, with a handful of cartridges.

It was not nearly as fine a weapon as Isham's .44 Colt. But it was smaller and lighter, easy to carry in his belt under a coat. He had long since decided he would not run from the man. If the bully wanted a fight, he could have it.

He was young and thought in terms of a fair fight. So he was surprised when he came down the front steps of his home one evening—and the bullet barely missed, possibly because of the poor light. He heard the shot and ducked as the heavy slug smashed the wood beside the door.

He dived into the shrubs that lined the walk as a second and third shot kicked up dirt around him.

The sniper was across the road where a line of trees marked the edge of brown fields. Reb crawled away from the front steps and found a place where he could see through the stalks, the revolver ready.

But no more shots came. He waited patiently, hoping to get a crack at the man, but saw nothing. His father came from the house with the shotgun and Reb rose from the shrubs, buttoning the coat over the pistol. He had told no one about buying it.

His father said, "Was someone shooting at you?"

"It was probably Willet." Reb showed him the bullet embedded in the door frame. "The shots came from across the street."

"Come on in the house."

In the morning they found evidence that someone had made himself comfortable under a clump of trees across from the house. Constable Jorganson's opinion was that the sniper had been Willet. "Who else, boy? You got any other enemies we don't know about?"

Todd said, "Of course he hasn't. What about those brass hats at the fort? Can't they control their men? I know the merchants and the saloon keepers want their trade, but they been shootin' up the town for years and it's time we put a stop to it."

"Yeah, I'll talk to them," Jorganson promised.

He talked to the mayor, Freeman Dietz, who sent a note to the fort's commanding officer, protesting the shooting.

"We can only do so much, dammit," Dietz told the constable. "Them soldiers spend one hell of a lot of money in this town. If we rile 'em up, they won't come here."

"We can't have 'em killin' our folks."

"You damn sure Reb didn't provoke that fight in the god-damn first place?"

"Real sure. Yes. Too many witnesses to be wrong. Besides, he's not a smart-ass kid. He could have killed them two and he didn't."

"All right. I'll tell that to the colonel."

The colonel sent Captain Thad Daniels to see the mayor. Daniels was middle-aged, a man grown stout and stodgy, a desk officer who had hopes of retiring one grade higher in another ten years.

"John Willet's record shows him to be a brawler, that's for sure," Daniels admitted. "Unfortunately, in peacetime we get those types. I understand you have only one policeman in the town."

"Yes. Name of Jorganson."

"Is he on duty day and night?"

Mayor Dietz smiled. "We don't have no crime here, Captain. He mostly watches the saloons."

"I see. Well, when our men are off duty, we cannot keep them from coming into town."

"So you're saying we got the problem."

Daniels nodded. "I'm afraid so. We will of course cooperate with you to the fullest. . . ."

The mayor sighed. "I guess we got to build us a jail."

"That might be wise. We will take our own off your hands as quickly as possible and put them in our stockade, but you will need a place to hold them. Men will become drunk and rowdy. It's human nature."

"It's not drinkin' I'm worryin' about, Captain. It's killin'."

Daniels grunted and stroked his chin. "Let's hope it doesn't come to that."

"I'm afraid it will."

3

There was no further incident for three weeks. Rebel turned seventeen in that time and continued working for Albe Newlan at the general store. He had gone through the local school, and if he wished to continue his studies, he would have to go to Berham.

He was aware his parents could not support him in another town, and from what he could glean the possibility of his getting a job there was not great.

When he talked with Lem Cotter, Lem said, "You've got two choices. Take the bull by the horns and go east—or stay here."

"People have two choices about everything—yes or no."

Lem grinned at him. "Very wise. So you decided what you want to do?"

Reb asked, "What about you?"

"I've decided to be a teacher. Next year I'll go to stay with relatives in Iowa. There's a school there and I'll get my teaching credential. . . ." He shrugged. "Then maybe come back here."

"To this little burg?"

"I like it here. What're you going to do?"

Reb shook his head. "I wish I knew." He rather envied Lem, who had his life planned out—except there was no excitement in it. No unknowns.

Since the attempted ambush in front of the house, Uncle Isham had taken him aside and pressed the .44 Colt into his hands. "It ain't necessary f'you to tell your mother about this, but I d'want you shot down in the goddamn street. At least this will give you a good chance to stay alive. Put it in your belt when you're outside at night."

"Thanks, Uncle Isham." Reb was delighted with the big revolver. He did not mention his smaller Smith pistol. He hid it in his room and left the Colt at the store except when he went home at night.

It was a dark night; the moon had a misty ring around it when he met Willet in the street. As soon as he saw the man Reb realized Willet had been waiting for him. The other had an ugly smile on his broad face. He stepped out from behind a tree to face Reb and, without a word, lifted a pistol.

Reb saw the sheen of it and instantly slid the Colt from his belt, drawing back the hammer as it came level. The two shots sounded almost together and Reb felt something prick at his sleeve. He saw Willet push around and sprawl face-down in the dirt. The gun went skittering away.

His heart hammering, he walked to the bluecoat. Willet did not move. Kneeling, Reb could see part of the other's face, eyes staring sightlessly. He felt for a pulse and there was none. Willet was dead.

Reb got up and took a long breath, shoving the pistol back into his belt. He tried to feel sorry for the man, but could not. He had come looking for trouble and had found it. Too bad.

Turning, he walked back into the town and rapped on the constable's door. Jorganson opened it, chewing on something. "Oh, hullo, Reb. What you want?"

Over the other's shoulder Reb could see the kitchen table set. Jorganson was in the middle of supper, probably preparing to go out on his rounds.

He said, "I just shot Willet."

"Where?"

"He's lying in the street back there." Reb leaned against the building, feeling tired. Jorganson hurried into the house and came out shoving into a coat. He had a lantern.

"Show me."

The body was just as he'd left it, on the edge of the dark street. Jorganson lifted the chimney and lighted the wick; he put the lantern down by Willet's face and felt for a pulse then shook his head. "Deader'n a carp."

"He was waiting for me," Reb said.

"What you shoot him with?"

Reb showed him the Colt. "It's my uncle Isham's. He gave it to me—in case."

Jorganson nodded. "Tell me what happened."

"He stepped out from behind that tree"—Reb pointed—"and fired at me. I fired back and he fell. That's about all."

"Isham tells me you're a dead shot with that thing."

"I'm sorry I had to shoot him."

Jorganson's brows lifted. "Willet was a sombitch. Don't feel sorry f'him. He got what was comin' to him." He chuckled. "Willet, he never figgered you'd have a shootin' iron on you. I 'spect he got one hell of a surprise, the poor dumb son of a bitch."

Two men had come out of a nearby house, gawking at the body in the street. The constable asked them for a wagon to haul the body away and one of them went toward the stable to get it.

Jorganson said, "You go on home, Reb. We don't need you here no more."

Reb nodded, feeling cold inside. The reaction was setting in. He had killed a man. . . . Of course the fight had been forced on him. He hadn't wanted to kill Willet. . . .

He was not particularly religious, though he had gone to church with his family for years, more or less the thing to do. The commandment Thou Shalt Not Kill occurred to him as he walked to the house. He stood outside looking up at the dark sky. An owl hooted somewhere off in the trees. Commandments had to be taken with a grain of salt, didn't they? If he hadn't shot Willet, he'd be dead now.

It didn't make him feel any better. He really was sorry the man had died like that, facedown in the dirt. Jorganson had called him a dumb son of a bitch.

He had been slow, too.

* * *

There had been no witnesses to the shooting. Willet had seen to that, picking a lonely spot. But his pistol had been fired and Reb had a tear in his coat. And he had told his story straightforward. The mere fact that Willet had been where he had been, waiting for his victim, said something.

Mayor Dietz and Jorganson were of a mind to call it quits. Everyone knew Willet had been the kind to want revenge. No one was in the least surprised that he had tried to get it and been centered instead.

But the army did not accept that. An official letter came from the commanding officer demanding a trial.

Since the town had no jail, Reb was turned over to his parents until the circuit judge should appear. That took a month.

In the meantime Reb was accosted at night by four men from the post. They came on him suddenly out of the dark, as Willet had done. He was perhaps a hundred yards from his own door when it happened. They came out of the gloom, silently, with clubs.

Reb saw the sudden movement and drew the Colt. He got off one shot that spun the attacker in front of him. He received a whack across the shoulders as he fell, firing again. Someone cursed and a club rattled on the roadway. A club reached his cheekbone, laying it open. He rolled and fired again and again, and they scattered, running into the dark.

The blows began to pain him. The club across his back had knocked him down, but at the same time had probably saved more hurt. He had fired up at them and had a fleeting impression of white teeth pulled back in a snarl.

They were gone and he lay still, on his back—it was good to lie quietly, getting his breath back. His cheek stung something fierce. He touched it gingerly and his fingers came away bloody. He began to hear voices from nearby houses. They had heard the shots.

He sat up and began reloading the gun.

Then lanterns came bobbing into the road and someone said, "Izzat you, Reb?"

"It's me. . . ."

His father bent over him. "Jesus, you're all bloody! What happened?"

Reb saw men clustered about a shapeless form in the road. Someone said, "He's dead."

Reb closed his eyes. He was sure he'd hit more than one of them. He said, "They came at me in the dark." There was blood in his mouth and he spit it out. His cheek hurt like hell!

Someone yelled that there was another one of them in the weeds across the road. "He dead, too."

His father lifted him, and Isham was there, helping him into the house where his mother bathed the wound and bandaged it gently. He heard her say, "This is going to leave a scar."

His back hurt. He wanted to tell them about it, but he was too tired to form the words. She gave him something hot to sip—it took forever too get it down, then he lay back. . . .

When he woke, it was morning, a gray dawn. He closed his eyes again, feeling the hurts. Those goddamn clubs had been murderous! They had probably wanted to beat him to death. Thank God for Colonel Colt.

When he opened his eyes again, Henry Jorganson was in the room. He stood by the bed, looking down. "How you feel, boy?"

Reb shook his head slightly. He hurt.

Jorganson smiled. "I think you look worse'n you are. How many of them was there?"

Reb held up four fingers.

"All soldiers?"

"I saw uniforms."

"Well, you got three of 'em. Two's dead and the third is shot up pretty bad. You keep that up and they going to have to send for more troops."

"Let him sleep, Henry," his mother said. "That's the best

thing for him." She brushed the hair off his forehead. "We'll get some soup into you in a while."

His cheek was a continual ache, but after he'd managed to swallow the hot soup, he felt better. It hurt to talk.

His father said, "The army came and hauled the three men away. Two are dead like Henry said. I reckon now the trial will be just a formality—if there is a trial."

The next days passed slowly. Reb stayed in the house with continual twinges in his back. It was difficult to get to sleep at night. He woke frequently, trying to find a spot where the back pains eased.

But the pains diminished gradually and his cheek healed, leaving a white scar from cheekbone to chin.

The circuit judge arrived in a black buggy with a skinny assistant, and Albe offered his store as a courtroom. There were half a dozen minor matters to be decided, but Reb's trial was the most important.

He had no lawyer—there was no lawyer in Rustin. The army had appointed a young lieutenant to handle its case.

The judge was a husky man with thinning gray hair and a courtly manner. His name was Hector Craddock. He sat behind a wooden table using a small mallet as a gavel. He had a no-nonsense face and he listened intently as the lieutenant stated the army's position.

He listened just as attentively to Reb and the other witnesses. He asked many questions, then nodded, tapping the gavel.

Reb had obviously acted in self-defense on both occasions concerning Willet, he declared. It was too bad Willet was dead, but he had probably gotten what was coming to him. People who go seeking trouble . . .

In the other matter, where Reb had been assaulted by four men, the judge took the army to task for not policing itself better. The attack by four men could only be construed as revenge. In his opinion, Craddock said, the surviving soldiers should be locked up for a very long time to contemplate their shortcomings. He wished he had the power to order it.

Reb was vindicated and free to go.

The gavel came down and the court was adjourned.

4

The army, however, did not take the judge's advice. Henry Jorganson was in the fort many times on other business and learned the two surviving men were only given company punishment—when one got out of the hospital. This kind of punishment was like slapping a wrist, Henry said. In his opinion they would try again.

Isham took Reb out into the open prairie to practice with the Colt. "Accuracy is the most important thing," Isham said. "But it don't hurt none to snake out a pistol quickly. A combination of the two might keep you alive."

Reb agreed that was to be desired.

He had no holster, so he wore the pistol in his belt and that occasioned a cross draw.

"Not a bad thing," Isham said. "Pull the gun and draw back the hammer as you turn it toward the target. You can practice that at home without firing."

Isham took along a gunnysack full of discarded food tins. He set them up, twenty-five paces distant, and Reb battered them into shreds, seldom missing a shot.

Then Isham tossed cans into the air, and after a short period of adjustment, Reb was able to hit every one. He was a dead shot.

After several practice sessions Isham told his brother-in-law, "Your boy can take care of himself. If them soldiers keep on comin' after him, I feel sorry for them."

"I don't want the boy to be a gunfighter."

"You don't want him dead neither. This is the only way

21

to make sure he stays alive. Sooner or later they'll realize they have to let him alone.''

"I hope you're right.''

Of the four soldiers who had attacked Reb, the two still alive brooded, talking constantly about how they would settle the score with the young kid in town. They heard Henry Jorganson brassing about what a dead shot the kid was, and they hesitated and kept talking.

One of the dead men, Perley Shinn, had a younger brother named Jerrol, who was not a soldier. Upon notification by the army, Jerrol had come to the post to view his brother's grave . . . and to ask about his brother's killer.

He was astonished to learn Reb was a seventeen-year-old boy. Jerrol was twenty-five and had spent his life among hard-living seamen. He considered himself tough as nails—and he was. He went into Rustin and spread the word in all the saloons that he was looking for Reb Wiley.

Henry Jorganson confronted Jerrol. "You ain't going to kill anyone in my town.''

"I was just joshin','' Jerrol said. "You going to arrest a man for talkin'?''

"I know who you are,'' Henry said. "You be on the stage tomorra.''

It took a very short time for Reb to hear the boast. A man was looking for him. Was he never going to see the end of these attacks?

They told him a man's brother had come to town—a man that Reb had killed. Did he have other brothers? How many would show up? Was Isham right, that if he stood up to them, the attacks would stop?

Reb slid the .44 Colt into his belt and walked into town. The brother was probably in a saloon. He took them one at a time.

When he got to the Senate Saloon at the edge of town,

Reb stepped inside. The long room was not crowded, only a dozen or so talking and drinking.

Reb said, "Is there somebody here named Jerrol Shinn?"

They all looked at him and the room grew silent.

Then a slim man stepped out to face him. "You must be that shitface kid who shot my brother."

"My name's Reb Wiley."

The other grimaced and went for his gun. Reb beat him, and his shot slammed the other back over a table. He crashed to the floor and lay still. Shinn's bullet went into the ceiling.

Someone felt for a pulse and looked at Reb. "He dead."

Henry Jorganson arrived within minutes, ordered Reb to go home and stay there, and questioned the witnesses. The body was dragged out to the boardwalk to await the undertaker.

The news of the shooting spread through the town seemingly in moments. The feud between Reb Wiley and soldiers from the fort had once more flared up, and a man was dead. Only this time the dead man was a civilian, a brother who had come to avenge a killing.

And there was one other difference: Reb had gone looking for a fight.

On hearing the news, Isham had hurried to the Wiley house. "We've got to get Reb out of town!"

"Why?" Todd asked. "It's those damn soldiers who keep after Reb. They won't let well enough alone. Everyone in town knows that this Jerrol Shinn said he was going to kill Reb."

"I know. But this time Reb went into the saloon asking for a fight. Reb pushed the other man into it."

Todd was surprised. He turned to look at his son. "Is that true?"

Reb nodded. "I knew it had to come to a fight." He made a face. "So I got it over with before he bushwhacked me."

"This time they've got a case," Isham said earnestly. "I'm

not arguing the merits of it—but they got a case. Let me take Reb to stay with George and Oralia. They won't find him there.''

"But he gave the man an even chance—'' Todd swung on Reb. "Didn't you?''

"Yes.''

"That doesn't matter. We can't trust any judge they send to be fair. The army is powerful. Any time you go to court it's chancy, no matter how right you are. The army's also got more money than we have. They could hire some fancy lawyer from the East and your son will be behind bars for years—maybe the rest of his life.''

Leona stood in the doorway and listened. She went to Reb and hugged him. "Take him there, Isham.''

Todd exclaimed, "If he runs away, it's like admitting guilt!''

"He's not running away,'' Isham retorted. "Not the way you mean. If he stays, he'll be crucified.''

"Isham is right,'' Leona said. "It's the only sensible thing to do. This thing has already gone too far. Those soldiers will never let him be . . . and sooner or later one of them will shoot Reb in the back.''

Todd sighed heavily, looked at his wife, and nodded. "All right. Get your things together, Reb.''

Henry Jorganson came to the house as Reb was packing a bag. He plunked down in a chair on the porch facing Isham and Todd. "I talked to them in the saloon. It was a fair fight—but Reb went a-lookin' for him, the Shinn feller.'' He fiddled with a cigar. "They can make somethin' out of that.''

"Who's 'they'?'' Isham demanded.

"The army of course. If they want to get into it. They got a couple of men dead and one crippled on account of Reb—no matter the truth of it.''

"We've just been talkin' about that,'' Todd said. "What if they can't find Reb?''

Jorganson smiled. "That's what I come over here t'say. You sending him away?''

Isham said, "Maybe."

The constable scratched a match and held it under the cigar. "If you are, don't tell me where." He got up and puffed smoke. "If the army sends that Captain Daniels over here again, I'll jus' tell 'im I can't find Reb." He grinned. "There ain't much they can do about that."

"Thanks, Henry." Todd nodded. "You figger they'll look for him?"

"I doubt it. Who's gonna do it?" He went down the steps.

It was a three-day journey across the prairie to the town of Haverford where George and Oralia Sims lived. George was Todd Wiley's first cousin.

He was also shiftless and usually unemployed.

Oralia was a long-suffering woman with a history of ailments and a whining voice. Nothing had ever gone right for her and she expected the future would be the same. It never occurred to her to try to change it.

Isham took George aside when they arrived, explaining the circumstances and that Todd would send him a little money each month to pay for Reb's keep . . . unless Reb got a job of course.

George's eyes lighted up at the mention of money and he agreed at once. "We got a spare room he can sleep in."

"Good. But don't spread it around that he's come here."

George frowned. "Is the law after him?"

"No, but we don't want to attract attention."

George grunted, wondering if he could keep the fact of the money from his wife, but decided he probably could not. If he did and she found out later, there would be hell to pay.

Reb was not impressed by his cousins, though he tried not to show it. He was given an attic room, the walls papered with newsprint. The single window was so grimy he could not see out. The rope bed was sagging and uncomfortable, and Oralia gave him blankets without sheets and a lumpy pillow.

He was a long way from home.

He had three dollars saved from his wages with Albe Newlan, and Isham had given him two dollars upon leaving. It would be enough to put himself into a hotel for a while—but what would he do when the money was gone?

The next morning he went out to look at the town. It was easily twice as large as Rustin, maybe three times. It was mostly a cow town and there was one saloon after another on the main street.

He went into three of them, asking for work, and was turned down. Then he got lucky. On one of the two side streets was a large barnlike structure with a sign: WAYLAND'S HAY GRAIN AND FEED. Below the large letters were smaller ones: *Bert Wayland, Prop*.

Bert Wayland was a man about sixty with white whiskers and a prominent belly. He wore a wide-brimmed straw hat on a bald head and looked at Reb with small round pop eyes.

"You live here in town, boy?"

"Yes, sir."

"I never seen you afore."

"I just came in. I'm staying with some cousins."

"You ain't leavin' tomorra?"

"No, sir. I can work. I'm strong."

"I can see you're strong. You know oats from hay?"

Reb smiled. "Yes, sir."

"What's your name?"

"Rebel Wiley."

"Rebel?"

"Well, my name's Rydal, but everyone calls me Reb."

"Ummm. That's nice and short. All right, Reb, I got a pile of chores. You fussy about what you do?"

"No, sir."

"All right. I give you fifty cents a day and I throw in one meal. That set good with you?"

"Fine, Mr. Wayland."

"And you stop callin' me sir. Ever'one calls me Bert."
He motioned. "Come on. I'll show you what I want
done."

5

There was a large dusty office just off the street in front of the barn. It was cluttered with a desk, several chairs, and some cabinets. It had been swept out about the time Betsy Ross had stitched her flag.

The rest of the barn was stalls, bins, shelves, and bags, all in confusing disarray. Bert explained that he had not been able to keep help, and what help he'd had in the past had not been worth the corn on his little toe. It was evident to Reb, as he listened to what the old man had to say, that Bert had no great expectations that Reb would be different.

However, he could see for himself what needed to be done and he pitched in. Inside a week he had the barn and the office straightened out and cleaned—to Bert's astonishment and pleasure. He even found things that Bert thought had been lost for years.

And when he had the barn in order, he made an inventory of goods and equipment, the first that Bert had seen in many years. He had been running his business in a hit-or-miss fashion for years and really did not know if he was making or losing money. The inventory allowed him to find out.

Behind the barn was a smaller building used as a stable. Reb swamped that out also and repaired a sagging door to the alley.

Each evening he went with Bert to his home, only a short walk across the alley and down. Bert's wife, Marian, was a slender, angular woman, very soft-spoken. She welcomed Reb, fed him as well as his own mother had, and asked innumerable questions about his home and family in Rustin. She was more curious than Bert why he had left home to come to Haverford, and he finally told her and Bert of his troubles with the soldiers. He had not left only because of himself, he said. He had worried that the soldiers would harm his family. With him gone, that was much less likely.

Marian thought it was terrible that a lad of his age should have to carry a pistol to defend himself in his own hometown.

"Sometimes the law ain't much," Bert said. "You can't depend on it for justice. They got their damn rules and to hell with anything else. My advice is to never go to court for anything. The damn fools they got for judges will rule agin you ever' time."

Red thought Bert must have had bad experiences with the law in the past. He did not argue.

In the following weeks business improved. The office was neat and clean, the barn was in excellent order with bins marked and easily accessible. Wagons came and went all day long; many customers said Bert's place was the best in town.

Bert doubled Reb's wages and gave him a horse, one of several he owned and kept in the stable with the two buggies he rented out.

Reb was delighted with the horse, a three-year-old bay, and rode out onto the prairie when he could get away, to practice with the Colt pistol.

Then Bert suggested he give up the attic room at George's and come to stay in the barn. "We can fix up a room f'you. What you say?"

Reb had already been thinking along those lines. He sketched plans and, when Bert approved, had lumber hauled in and framed a room at the rear of the building. He put in a floor, walls and ceiling, a door, and two windows with glass. Bert was happy to pay for the materials; now he would have someone on the premises all the time. He confided to Marian that it had been his lucky day when Reb had showed up asking for work.

* * *

Reb kept very busy and six months went by quickly. He received several letters from his mother in that time and had written back.

Then one day he received a letter from his father. That in itself was a startling occurrence. It was a short note; his father came right to the point. Reb's mother was ailing and it might be a very good idea for him to return home at once.

He showed the letter to Bert, who had his wife pack some food. He was on the trail to Rustin, on the bay horse, within an hour.

He arrived home only minutes before his mother died. He had barely taken hold of her small white hand when she slipped away. He knew she had recognized him and smiled. . . .

His father and Isham sat in the parlor in tears. The doctor filled out his papers and left and Reb walked out into the night, all the memories of his childhood crowding in on him, each one concerned with her. Somehow he hadn't thought of losing her; she had always been there.

Twenty or more people were at the graveside, standing solemnly in a cold wind as the minister intoned the service. Reb stood by his father and Isham, head down, not wanting to look at the black-painted pine box.

Her passing made great changes. Todd and Isham decided one of them would put his home up for sale—it was finally Isham—and the two men would live in one house, sharing expenses. It was foolish to keep two homes.

There had been no further violence from soldiers at the fort and Todd suggested his son might safely return home now.

Lying in bed in his old room, Reb thought about it. Did he want to return? He had begun to make a life for himself in Haverford with the Waylands. Of course he was only eighteen yet. . . . But Bert had hinted that one day he would want to retire and take it easy, and perhaps Reb might buy him out. No such opportunity existed in Rustin. His father and Isham still talked about getting a herd of cattle together, but they had done nothing about it.

He was beginning to realize they never would.

There were few changes in the little town; Albe was delighted to see him, and the news of his returning seemingly took only minutes to reach everyone. When he came out of Albe's store, several soldiers passed by and stared at him.

Then two days after the funeral shots were fired into the Wiley house late at night, breaking windows and smashing dishes on a shelf.

Reb was not forgotten.

Uncle Isham insisted he return to Haverford as quickly as possible. ''We don't want to see you killed!''

Todd said heavily, ''Apparently they have long memories.'' He shook his head, looking at his son. ''It might be best, for another year or so.''

Reb was of two minds about leaving. He had decided to go back to Haverford, but he did not want to seem afraid to stay.

Henry Jorganson came to the house and helped with his decision. ''The soldiers jabber about shooting Reb—when they're drinking. And sooner or later one of 'em will, or try to. They're still all stirred up about last year. If Reb shoots another one of 'em, it'll just get worse.''

Reb said, ''I don't want to run away.''

Jorganson chewed on a pipe stem. ''What I think is—if they can't get you, they'll come after your pa. They already fired into the house. They didn't do that when you was away.''

Reb nodded, chewing a lip. It was a situation that could not be won. The army could not control its off-duty men and neither could the town constable. He was only one, after all, up against so many.

So what it came down to was that Isham was right. It was time to go. Otherwise his family would suffer.

He packed his bag again; he would leave at sunup. In the evening after dark he walked into town to say good-bye to Albe Newlan and spent an hour in the store talking and eating walnuts.

When he left the store, it was full dark—and they were

waiting for him. Three blue-clad soldiers from the fort, spaced out across the dirt street.

Reb stood on the boardwalk, three steps above the street, and gazed at them, feeling his blood racing. The .44 Colt was in his belt under the coat, the bulk of it very comforting. He did not recognize any of the three and he was slightly surprised to find himself very cool and deliberate, though his pulse rate had changed.

He let them make the first move.

The man to his left suddenly raised his arm, with a pistol in his hand. As he fired Reb jumped to the street and flattened himself on the ground, the .44 leaping into his grip. How many times had he done this on the prairie? He fired and rolled and fired again. The other two were banging shots at him—one was down. Then another fired into the dirt and sat down, facing away. Reb fired twice at the third man, who turned and ran, dropping his weapon. He stumbled and fell, tried to get up, and finally lay, kicking one leg.

It was over in seconds. A dozen or more shots had been fired in quick succession. Many had rapped into the building behind him. Reb got up slowly and reloaded the Colt, gritting his teeth. He was untouched.

He walked to the man on his left. Dead. The sitting man was slumping lower and Reb kicked his pistol away.

A half-dozen men appeared, some with lanterns. Then Henry Jorganson came running and Albe Newlan emerged from the store, wringing his hands. He called to Reb, "Are you all right?"

Reb nodded. He said to Jorganson, "Three of them were waiting for me."

"Them goddamned soldiers!" Henry went to the sitting man. Two others with lanterns had laid him down. He had a bullet in his middle and was coughing blood. A half-dozen troopers from the saloons stood around, growling between themselves, staring at Reb.

Reb stood on the boardwalk, the coat pulled back so he could reach the pistol quickly, and watched them.

The third man was dead, too, three bullets in him.

Someone brought a buckboard and the two bodies were lifted in. The doctor had been called and advised not moving the wounded man. He took Jorganson aside. "He won't make it through the night."

Jorganson fiddled with a pipe and talked to Reb. "Best you git the hell out of town. They going to bushwhack you sure's hell got an iron floor."

"I'll be gone by morning."

"Don't tell me nothing. All's I got to know is these three fools was waitin' for you when you come out of the store. Albe says that's what happened. And they got what they was lookin' for—trouble."

"It's not going to stop, is it?"

"No, it ain't. Not as long as you stay here in Rustin."

His father and Isham came walking into the circle of lantern light. Isham carried his carbine. "What happened?"

Jorganson told them and Todd shook his head, watching the soldiers straggle back to the saloon.

The constable said, "I been listening to a lot of talk. Them soldiers can't believe a boy can stand them all off and kill four, five of them."

"Reb's not stayin' in town."

Henry nodded. "He told me." He squinted at Reb. "I think you oughta go tonight—and watch your back."

6

Reb left after midnight, walking and leading the bay horse, his .44 in hand. But he met no one. A goodly distance from the house he mounted and took the road to Haverford without incident.

He arrived on Sunday when the barn was closed. He put the horse in the corral and Bert showed up in an hour to insist he come to the house for supper; Marian would be delighted to see him.

Reb did not mention the fracas in Rustin, knowing it would only upset them, even though he had come out of it without a scratch.

He said nothing to anyone about the fight, but the fact that he had killed those men, even in fair fights, weighed heavily upon him. He was not concerned with burning forever in hell as some preachers threatened, but he did muse about the hereafter now and again. Would he be called to account and have to stand trial again—in a much higher court?

Three days after he returned to Haverford the local weekly came out. That afternoon Reb heard Bert yell in the office and went hurrying to the door, "What is it?"

Bert shook the paper. He looked over his glasses accusingly. "It says here you had a fight in Rustin!"

"It does?" Reb sat down facing the other.

"It says you had a fight with three soldiers and kilt them all! Izzat true?"

Reb sighed deeply. "They were waiting for me when I

came out of the store. They were looking for trouble." Bert knew about the other fights.

Bert grunted and folded the paper. "It don't say where you are now, but it gives your name." He stabbed the paper with a stubby finger. "It says here you're holdin' an entire fort full of soldiers at bay."

"That's ridiculous." Reb shook his head. "I can't be held responsible for what some newspaper says. Besides, I'm not in Rustin now. And I didn't look for those fights—except one, and that was only to keep from being shot in the back."

Bert nodded and put the paper aside. "Well, maybe nobody much knows your name here in town. In a week it could all blow over."

Reb got up. "Let's hope it does."

But it did not.

A good many townspeople had been in the barn and had talked to Reb about one thing and another, and many remembered him—and his name. It could not be kept secret.

The lurid piece in the newspaper was talked about in the saloons, but no one did anything but talk—except Curly Bisch.

Curly was a young tough who worked, when he worked, at breaking horses. He had survived a number of saloon gunfights and was now given a wide berth by most because he had a quick temper and was known to be slick with a gun.

He very much enjoyed his modest reputation and hungered to increase it. It was important to him that men made way for him when he entered a saloon. Bartenders hurried to serve him, with smiles. When he sat in on a card game, Curly was treated with deference.

So when Curly heard about the young kid Reb Wiley, and heard men discussing him with what seemed to be respect, it bothered him. It was almost as if the kid had deliberately tried to outdo him. He came to hate Reb without ever having seen or met him.

And it was worse when he heard the kid worked in a feed barn doing manual labor. It disgusted him to hear the kid had stood off soldiers, and killed some of them. How could all that be true!

And then one evening Curly walked by the barn to find the kid leaning on a rake in the doorway, looking at the sky.

Curly stopped in front of him. "You that kid they call Reb?"

Reb looked at him, noting the swagger, the holstered revolver, the sneering voice. It was not unusual for men to wear guns, although most did not in the town unless they had just come in. But this one probably wore his all the time. There was a certain look to him. He probably fancied himself something very special.

Reb said, "Who's asking?"

Curly flushed and sudden anger impelled him. He stepped forward to slap some sense into the smartmouthed young kid—and suddenly had a rake handle under his chin, snapping his head back. Then almost instantly something very hard hit the side of his head and he collapsed in a shower of colored lights and bright stars.

He could not believe he was lying in the dirt, flat on his back, blinking, trying to clear his head . . . which hurt abominably. He grabbed at his pistol and found the holster empty. With considerable effort he sat up and saw the kid—still leaning on the rake, and with the pistol in his belt.

Reb said conversationally, "Your name is Curly Bisch, isn't it?"

Curly got to his feet unsteadily, raging mad. He put his head down and charged suddenly. Somehow his feet got tangled with the rake handle and he was hit again alongside the head. This time he fell facedown, tasting dirt. He had a terrible pain throbbing in his head. It seared him and his eyes didn't focus properly. What the hell had hit him?

He managed to roll over and sit up, feeling dizzy. He heard Reb say, "Here's your gun."

The kid threw the pistol into the street, fifty or sixty feet away. He was leaning on the rake again when Curly got to his feet, reeling a bit.

A half-dozen men were standing on the boardwalk not far off, watching.

Curly slapped dirt from his clothes. His hat was in the middle of the street. He picked it up, stumbling a little. He was going to kill that kid for sure.

He found his gun in the mud beside a water trough. He swore, wiping the mud off; the barrel was filled with it. He glared at the watchers and plodded down the street toward his boardinghouse. The kid would pay. . . .

Bert Wayland came out of the office white-faced. He had seen the entire thing and pulled Reb into the barn. "He's going to kill you for that! Did you have to knock him down with everyone watching?"

Reb said reasonably, "He was going to knock me down."

Bert sighed. "He won't give you a chance!"

Reb stood the rake in a corner. "Stop worrying, Bert. I won't fight him if I don't have to."

"You damn fool, Reb! I know his kind. He can't let it go! Not with people watching him get dumped in the street like that. You took his gun away and he'll never forgive you for it." He paced the office. "Maybe you ought to go away for a while—maybe Curly will leave town."

Reb laughed. "I came *here* to get away from people like Curly. Now you want me to move on?"

"Reb, dammit! I want you to stay alive!"

"I intend to."

He knew how Bert felt, and he thought about it when he was alone, about going somewhere else. But deep down he hated to do it. He certainly did not fear Curly Bisch and he was not going to let the man run him away.

And he knew Curly would come after him. He did not know when, so he kept the .44 handy.

Curly made threats against Reb in the saloons. The smart-mouthed kid's luck was going to run out. He'd had all the luck he was going to get—except the bad kind.

And someone in the back of the saloon hollered, asking

him when he was going to fix the kid's wagon, and Curly felt himself badgered.

"Right now," he said angrily, and stalked out of the saloon.

He walked to the feed barn with the crowd trailing him, jabbering among themselves with a growing excitement. Curly was going to provoke a fight. The crowd grew in numbers as it approached the barn.

It was late afternoon of a spring day. Reb heard them coming and guessed immediately what was occurring. He flicked open the loading gate of the Colt and rolled the cylinder down his arm, looking at the brass. Six beans in the wheel. He slid the pistol into his belt and walked to the door, his jaw tight.

Bert Wayland was standing in the wide doorway, talking to the crowd, telling them to bust it up and go on home. But when they saw Reb, the chatter increased. Bert turned. "Dammit, Reb, stay back in there!"

Reb pushed past him, looking for Curly. The crowd suddenly parted, getting out of the line of fire; men scrambled, staring at him.

Curly stood in the middle of the street, scowling, thumbs hooked in his cartridge belt.

Someone grabbed Bert and hauled him to one side, still protesting. Reb halted, looked at Curly, and smiled.

Then Curly went for his gun.

The gun barely cleared leather before Reb's shot centered him. Curly's finger jerked on the trigger and the pistol fired once into the dirt, then he crumpled to sprawl like a sack of rags. His hat rolled away and the crowd seemed to sigh as one.

Someone knelt and felt for a pulse. There was none.

Curly had no friends who were of a mind to continue the feud with Reb. At least no one looked Reb up to call him out. He was gaining a reputation as one quick hombre.

"It's the last thing I need," Reb told Bert. "I don't want to be known as a gunfighter."

"I'm afraid it's too late for that." Bert shook his head sadly. "It's bein' forced on you. You're lucky folks didn't care much for Curly, but if it had been someone else . . ."

The town law, in the person of Nick Bowles, came 'round to see him. Nick had been away in the East for a week and had missed the quarrel. He was an old-timer, lean as a reed and weather-beaten. He wore striped pants and a black vest with a star pinned to it. He sat in Bert's office and chatted as though nothing had happened.

When Reb entered, he got up and Bert introduced them. Reb said politely, "Glad to meet you, Marshal."

"So you're the one they call Reb."

Reb smiled. "Yes, sir. It's a nickname I picked up a long time ago."

"Where'd you learn to handle a gun?"

"From my father and uncle."

"I understand you were having some problems with soldiers."

"Yes, sir. That's why my uncle gave me the gun." He looked at Bert. "I just locked the stable for the night."

Bert nodded.

Reb said to the marshal, "Did you come to arrest me?"

"No." Bowles sat. "Nothin' to arrest you for. I didn't see the fight, but they tell me Curly come down here looking for trouble."

"He sure as hell did!" Bert said loudly. "He only got what was comin' to him." He grinned. "I bet he was one surprised son of a bitch, too."

Nick laughed. "Which side're you on, Bert?"

When Reb had left them, Nick said, "Seems like a right sociable boy."

"The Lord never made a harder-workin' lad. The trouble is, folks picks on him, like them soldiers did over to Rustin. Reb never starts no trouble, but he can sure as hell finish it. He's quick as spilled milk and he's a dead shot."

Nick made a wry face. "That's a might starchy combination. Be better for him, likely, if he didn't know one end of a gun from t'other." He shrugged. "But that's rain already in the barrel. I have to tell you, though, they talking about him in the town.''

''Who's talking?''

''A few of the mealymouths. Some get their feathers up when they got a few drinks in 'em. I just hope they don't come down here to call Reb into the street.''

''So do I.'' Bert blew out his breath. ''So do I.''

No one came to yell for Reb, but two nights later a shot was fired into the office, barely missing Bert as he sat at his desk preparing to lock up and go home.

Reb came running with the .44 and looked everywhere along the street but found no one.

In his room that night he worried over it. The same thing that had happened in Rustin had finally followed him here. If he stayed, Bert might be killed. Some half-drunk picker might decide that shooting Bert would be the same as harming Reb.

It was time to move on.

7

He discussed packing up and going the next morning with
Bert, who was of two minds about it. He wanted Reb to be
safe, but he hated to see him leave.

"Where will you go?"

"I don't know . . . but that's not important. I've always
wanted to see the country, so this is a good excuse to do it.
I'll let the road decide."

"Will you let us know how you are?"

"Of course."

Marian Wayland was glad that he was taking himself out
of danger—neither of them had told her about the shot into
the office. There would be another one like Curly Bisch along
at any time, she said. And the next one might shoot him in
the back.

He tied his bedroll behind the cantle, hung on a war bag
containing his slicker, another shirt, and some airtights, said
good-bye to Bert, and mounted the bay horse. He felt as if
he were leaving home again.

He did not ride through Haverford, to advertise his going,
but cut across back lots to gain the road to Wenger. It was
largely a stage road, though he did not meet the stage during
the two days it took to reach the town.

Wenger was on the flats, at the foot of a cactus-covered,
jagged hill. There were saloons, stores, and wagon yards
along the angled street, and nearby, close to a wandering
stream, were the tepees of a few horse Indians.

41

It was a chilly day when Reb got down in front of the BeeHive Saloon and, drawing the coat tightly about him, went inside. The room was nearly empty. A bartender was playing cards at the end of the long bar with a well-dressed man in a bowler hat.

Reb ordered beer. "Anybody hiring hereabouts, you know of?"

The other squinted at the amber-colored window. "You might try Dustin's. It's a freighting outfit. They got men coming and going all the time." He jerked his thumb. "You see the sign down at the end of town."

"Thanks."

Dustin's Freighting had a big weathered sign over the wide gate. Inside were buildings, wagons, a blacksmith shop, and off to the right, a line of corrals where mules waited.

A crudely lettered sign over a door read: OFFICE. Reb got down and went inside to find two clerks with eyeshades sitting at desks with ledgers and papers spread about. One glanced at him and Reb said, "I'm looking for work."

"You'll have to see Mr. Dustin. He's outside there somewhere. Just ask anybody."

"Thanks."

He went into the yard, asked a few questions, and was directed to the owner, Dustin, who was watching men repair a wagon wheel. Dustin was middle-aged, getting gray about the temples, with a full, ruddy face and bushy brows. He turned when Reb appeared.

"You Mr. Dustin, sir?"

"Yes . . ."

"I'm looking for work."

Dustin nodded and squinted at him. "What can you do?"

Reb smiled. "Whatever needs to be done."

"You drive a big wagon?"

"Yes, sir." Driving a wagon required very little experience. In fact, most drivers walked a good bit of the time.

Dustin nodded again. "All right. You go over to the warehouse there and see Wade Colter. If he's not in there, he'll

be at the blacksmith shop. Tell 'im you're on the payroll.
Twenty-five dollars a month.''

"Yes, sir.''

Wade Colter was a skinny, long-faced man with slitted
eyes in a mass of wrinkles. He listened to Reb, nodded, and
said, ''We making up a train, expect to shove out in a day'r
two for the far sticks, maybe less if we git 'em loaded. You
start in the mornin'. Five o'clock sharp. That all right?''

"That's fine, sir.''

"Folks calls me Wade. You got a gun?''

Reb opened the coat to show the .44.

Wade said, ''You got a rifle, too?''

"No. D'you expect Indian trouble?''

"Always have to expect it. We got a few extry Winchesters. Can you shoot perty good?''

"Yes.''

Wade squinted at him and nodded.

He rode into the yard just before five the next morning and
saw the line of wagons standing in the road, each one with a
team of mules in harness.

Wade motioned to him. ''Pull off the saddle and hang'er
in the barn.'' He pointed. ''Put that bay in the near corral.
He'll be taken care of while you're gone.''

"Which wagon do I drive?''

"You're new, so you take one of them in the rear.''

Reb did as he was told and slung his war bag into the next
to last wagon. It was crammed with boxes and barrels. Apparently a crew had worked in the night hours to load up.

He stayed by the wagon watching the organized confusion
as Wade and a few others, including clerks from the office,
attended to last-minute details. Then Dustin came out of the
office with a heavy green folder, which he gave to Wade.
The two talked for a few minutes then Dustin returned to the
office and Wade dropped the folder in the lead wagon and
cupped his hands: ''Let's roll on!''

He mounted a roan horse and they were on their way. Reb
hadn't asked where.

He found out the first evening.

The wagon train was on its way to Fort Canfield with supplies and equipment, a long way out in the wilderness.

As they sat around a fire that night another man, Tim Foley, who was Reb's age, said, "It'll take us weeks to get there. You figgerin' to get rich driving a wagon?"

"Well, if it takes a month each way, I'll have fifty dollars when I get back. I don't have that now."

Tim grinned. "You sure as hell can't spend it out here, if you did have it. 'Less you're a gambler."

"What about Indians?"

Tim shrugged. "I only been with one other outfit and we didn't see any. But they say the Kiowas are the worst. The old-timers say their war parties drift all over the damn landscape looking for whatever. They're fierce fighters. I hope we don't meet any."

"Me either."

Wade came riding up to the wagon the next morning and handed Reb a well-used Winchester and a sack of cartridges. "You're signed out for this, Reb. Take care of it or it comes out of your pay."

"All right."

"It shoots a little bit to the right or left, I forget which. Take a few shots when we stop."

Reb smiled. "All right."

The freighting outfit consisted of twenty-six wagons and drivers and a half-dozen herders and extra hands, not counting Wade. Tim Foley thought it likely that an Indian band might pass them by as having too much firepower. Every man had a rifle and most had six-guns, too.

The days passed slowly and tediously leading into summer. The days lengthened into weeks. They saw moving specks in the far distance many times that Wade declared were Indians watching them, but non came near.

Then finally Fort Canfield was close by, the scouts told them. They trailed through the wide gates without incident and the wagons were unloaded into the quartermaster's building.

The fort was situated on a low bluff overlooking a wide stream and was long-established, though most of the original buildings had been replaced, rebuilt with milled lumber, and the whole no longer had a log palisade.

They did not linger at the fort. Wade allowed the men baths and a chance to buy necessities; then, when the wagons were unloaded, he had the train on the road again, saying they could make no money with empty wagons.

He did not lead them back the way they had come, but headed for the town of Hicourt, where he expected to pick up a cargo bound for Wenger.

But it was at Fort Canfield, while the men were enjoying the bath house, that someone noticed the item in a discarded newspaper, many weeks old, concerning Reb. Everyone in the wagon train knew about the Curly Bisch shooting within hours.

Tim Foley said, "Was that you, Reb?"

He had to admit it. "He pushed me into the fight."

"Jesus! They say you're a gunslick!"

"The world is full of 'theys.' "

Tim said, "I notice you always got that forty-four in your belt."

"It's so another Curly won't try me. Maybe the next one will back off."

They rolled into Hicourt in the early afternoon, a dusty little settlement on the high plains. They trailed through and bivouacked just outside the town in a flat meadow. Wade immediately went to palaver with the town merchants.

The drivers wandered into town at once, to visit the saloons. When they were gone, Tim Foley motioned to Reb. "Lookit this."

He unfastened a piece of tarpaulin that had been snugged down tight over boxes in his wagon. "They didn't deliver all the load in Fort Canfield."

Reb was surprised. "Are these the same crates that were loaded in Wenger?"

"Look at the markings! They're consigned to Canfield."

"Let's look in the other wagons."

There were partial loads in five other wagons—all of goods consigned to Fort Canfield.

"What does it mean?" Tim asked.

"It means that the army is paying for goods it didn't receive." Reb scratched his chin. "Who's doing it, Wade or Dustin? If these wagons aren't unloaded before we get back to Wenger, then Dustin is in on it, too."

"And so is someone at the fort."

"That's right. It would have to be. Someone had to sign for everything. They've got a fancy piece of larceny going here. Wade takes part of the cargo back and they sell it and divide the profits—and send the man at the fort his share."

Tim said, "And Dustin hauls to other forts, too. He could be doing the same thing with them."

"Keep it under your hat," Reb advised, "until we get back to Wenger."

"What've you got in mind when we get there?"

"I dunno. I'll sleep on it."

They picked up cargo in Hicourt, and in another town, Medina, they loaded ten wagons with whitened bones that would be shipped east and ground up for fertilizer.

In Wenger, Reb returned the unused rifle and the men were paid off. Nearly all disappeared into town. Reb saddled the bay horse and walked out of the stable to find Wade and several others unloading the Canfield-assigned boxes and hauling them into the warehouse.

Reb paused and Wade motioned him to go on. "You got your time. You're through here."

Reb leaned on the horse, annoyed. "Does stealing pay pretty good, wagon boss?"

Wade paled, then his face flushed and he jumped at Reb— halting abruptly as he stared into the muzzle of the Colt.

"You son of a bitch! Git outta this yard!"

Reb swung up into the saddle without a word. He turned

the bay's head and rode out quickly, loping into town. He had probably overplayed his hand. Now Wade, and Dustin too, knew he was aware of their scheme, and might suppose he would go to the law about it.

He could expect they would try to kill him to shut his mouth. Why did trouble stick to him like a cocklebur?

In town he met Tim Foley in the Paradise Saloon. They sipped beer and he told Tim what had occurred in the yard.

"You best hustle your ass out of town," Tim said. "They going to get you for that."

It was probably very good advice, moving on. But he could not bring himself to follow it. He could not let a bunch of crooks chase him away. He had only left Rustin because of the possible harm to his family. And he had left Haverford because the same thing might happen to Bert and his wife.

There were none of those reasons here in Wenger.

He had no idea how many Wade and Dustin could array against him. Most, he thought, would not backshoot a man, and most were not gunfighters. So maybe Wade could scrape up three or four willing to do battle with one man—and he had faced those odds from the soldiers.

When he left Tim, he went across the street to the hotel and signed for a room. He took his bedroll up and tossed it on a bunk. The room had a single, grimy window and he looked out over rooftops. Smoke was drifting lazily from chimneys. He didn't care to be chased out of town, but he didn't want to stay either. Wenger had nothing for him.

He decided he would get a good night's sleep and leave in the morning. The next town west was Gainesville; maybe he could find a job there.

He spread the blankets and stretched out.

He woke in two hours and sat up. It was getting dark out and he was hungry. He slipped into his coat and went downstairs to the street. He'd noticed a restaurant close by.

As he stepped off the boardwalk a man came toward him from the opposite side and halted, facing him. The man was slim, wearing fancy striped pants, a crisp white shirt, black coat and hat. His pistol was in a leather holster, tied down snug alongside his leg.

Reb knew instantly he was a gunman.

8

Reb halted, facing the other; there was maybe thirty feet between them. The man said, "Your name Reb?"

Curly Bisch had asked the same thing. Reb said, "Who wants to know?" He opened his coat.

"My name's Hinch."

"Who's paying you?"

Hinch did not reply. Instead, he went for his gun. He was very swift and he got off one shot. It slammed into the dirt halfway between them. Reb's shot knocked him backward and the gun went skittering away.

Reb did not move. He flicked open the loading gate and ejected the spent brass, shoving another shell into the chamber. Several bystanders ran into the street and bent over the downed man. One looked back at Reb. "He's gone."

Reb nodded and went on to the restaurant.

He felt almost nothing but relief that it was over. Hinch meant less than nothing to him . . . like shooting at the cans his uncle Isham had tossed into the air. Hinch was merely an obstacle, hired by Dustin to do his dirty work.

Tomorrow he would deal with Dustin.

He sat at a side table and ate beefsteak and no one came near him but the waiter. He saw their faces, staring at him. Apparently Hinch had enjoyed a reputation—and now that rep was his.

When he returned to the hotel, the body had been taken away and Tim Foley was waiting for him. "Do you know who you shot?"

"He said his name was Hinch."

"Yeah. Peter Hinch. They say he was the most dangerous man in the territory."

"Is that so? I figured he was hired by Dustin." He looked at Tim quizzically. "Does Wade know you saw those crates, too?"

"I never told him I did." Tim shrugged.

"Then you better not be seen with me. It might give them ideas."

He rode to the Dustin Freight Yard the next morning and got down in front of the office. Pulling the .44, he kicked open the door and the two clerks stared at him white-faced.

Reb said, "Where's Dustin?"

"I-I-I d-dunno," one stammered.

The yard was cluttered with wagons. He went past them to the long warehouse. As he entered from the sunlight shots slammed into the wall near him from somewhere in the dim interior.

Reb ducked, hearing retreating footsteps. He jumped up and fired at a moving shadow. It was dark and close; there were stacks of boxes and crates to the ceiling, with black-painted numbers. He heard a door slam at the back and ran down a center aisle.

He opened the rear door and jumped out quickly—and halted. Dustin was spurring a horse away, heading for the town. There was no chance for a shot.

He went into the warehouse, looking for Wade. Several workers told him they hadn't seen Wade for a bit. He looked into all the buildings and sheds without turning the man up. There were a hundred places to hide and Wade would know them all. He mounted the bay horse and rode back to town.

Tim met him in the stable behind the hotel. "What happened?"

"Dustin ran out, and so did Wade."

"They heard what happened to Hinch."

"I suppose so."

Tim said, "While you were gone I had a talk with the

deputy here in town. I told him what we'd seen in Dustin's wagons—and what we suspected. I also told him that was probably why Hinch tried to kill you yesterday. Hinch was paid by Dustin.''

Reb smiled. ''You've been busy.''

''Well, I was afraid they'd dry-gulch you at the yard—so at least they wouldn't get away with it.''

''What will the deputy do about it?''

''He said he'd forward a report to the sheriff, and the sheriff would probably send it to the U.S. marshal because the army was involved. Then they'd make their own investigation.''

Reb nodded. ''Good.''

''What're you going to do now?''

''Think I'll go on to Gainesville, see what I can find there.''

''A job? You want some company?''

''Come along.''

They left Wenger at noon and arrived in Gainesville two days later at dusk. It was a cow town in a pleasant valley that was partly forested. It had white-picket-fenced houses and a weekly newspaper, the *Democrat*. Tim picked up a copy; the Hinch shooting was on the front page.

Hinch was described as the man who had shot three members of the notorious Coleman gang and who had survived a dozen gunfights. But he had been bested by a youngster, Reb Wiley, who had been involved in numerous fights with soldiers in Rustin.

Hinch had been buried in the local boot hill. His epitaph read: *Here Lies Peter Hinch. He Had a Slow Day*.

Reb laughed, reading it. It was inevitable, of course, that the incident should be reported; he was thankful that he'd never had a photograph taken. It was bad enough that they knew his name.

There were three boardinghouses in Gainesville and he and Tim found rooms in one of them.

But there were few jobs to be had. Reb had no experience

as a cowhand and no inclination to spend his days on the range. Tim Foley had some schooling and was good with figures; he hoped to find work as an accountant.

Reb went to see the local lawman when nothing else turned up. The law was a deputy sheriff named Homer Bennett whom most called HB. He was a well-set-up man with brown hair and an easy manner. His helper had just gotten married, he said, and gone off to live in another town. He needed someone to take his place.

"You ever been a lawman?"

"No, but I learn quickly."

HB frowned. "Your name is Reb Wiley? Where'd I hear that name lately?"

Reb sighed. "It's been in the papers."

HB snapped his fingers. "You're the man who shot Hinch!"

"I'm afraid so."

"Ahhh." HB looked at Reb more closely. "Most gunfighters are gamblers. Do you gamble?"

"Seldom." Reb smiled. "I'm not a gunfighter."

"Was Hinch facing you in that fight?"

"Yes, certainly."

"Did you draw against him?"

Reb nodded.

HB grinned. "Then you're what you are."

He was hired as a helper and HB gave him a badge to wear. HB had a schedule, when each would make rounds in the town. The merchants liked to see a star now and then during the day, he said. Reb could start the next morning.

It proved to be an easy job. The town had no crime. It had a few drunks, especially on Saturday nights, but even those gave Reb no trouble. He escorted them to the jailhouse and left them to sleep off whatever poison they had sopped up. As soon as they were sober and paid a small fine, he let them go.

Tim Foley secured a job taking care of the accounts of a cattle ranch out of town, and the days passed.

And as they passed, Reb began to notice that HB was more and more out of touch. When he asked the deputy about it, HB said, "Private business, Reb."

"What kind of private business?"

"Can I depend on you to say nothing about this? I don't want it to get back to the sheriff."

The sheriff was a hundred miles away. Reb nodded.

"All right. I'm doing some horse trading—buying and selling horses, and a few mules." HB shrugged. "I don't intend to remain a deputy all my life, and one of these days when I get a business going, I'll resign."

That seemed reasonable enough.

Reb spent several hours each day in the small office and, to ward off tedium, began to go through the stack of wanted posters, some yellowing with age. He did not expect to find any of the wanted men in Gainesville—but one never knew. He read each of the dodgers carefully.

He knew where HB conducted most of his business, an isolated barn with several corrals. Reb had been on the job a month when he happened by the barn one afternoon. He found HB sitting on a top rail contemplating half a dozen horses in the corral.

"What you doing here, Reb?"

"Just making my rounds. Are these your horses?" Two or three of them were really fine animals. One was a particularly beautiful bay gelding with a glistening black mane and tail, branded Bar H-O. His own bay could not compare with it.

"Just bought the bunch," HB said, climbing down. "Figger to sell 'em this afternoon."

When he returned to the office, Reb sat at the desk, staring out at the street. What was nagging at his memory? He had seen something . . . what was it?

He got out the posters and went through them and suddenly one jumped out at him—Bar H-O! Half a hundred Bar H-O horses had been stolen weeks ago!

The bay he'd seen had been the only horse bearing that

brand. Did HB know it was a stolen animal? When the deputy came to the office later, Reb showed him the poster.

HB whistled. "I didn't know that! And them horses are forty miles away from here by now." He snapped his fingers. "I'll go send a telegram." He rushed out.

More because of curiosity than anything else, Reb kept a watch on that corral. It was outside the town in an area of shacks and barns. He saw HB there several times, often talking with men he'd never seen before. There were usually horses in the corral.

Several days after he'd shown HB the poster Reb noted horses in the corral and got a close-up look at them when HB was away. Two were branded Bar H-O.

Reb borrowed a pair of field glasses from the office desk and watched the corral from a distance where he could not be seen. HB appeared with two strangers. They examined the horses and money was passed to HB and the horses were led away. Probably to be rebranded.

So HB knew they were stolen!

What to do about it? Could he turn his back and walk away from obvious thievery? He hated thieves. And if he let it go, wouldn't it get worse? Undoubtedly.

Finally he sent a telegram to the sheriff to say that horse stealing was going on and asked the sheriff to come to Gainesville himself to take charge of the case. He also asked the sheriff to say nothing to anyone about it.

But he did. The sheriff sent a wire to HB saying he was on his way to investigate the horse-stealing charge brought by Reb.

9

When he received the sheriff's telegram, HB was enraged.
The damned kid, still wet behind the ears, was accusing him!
He drew his six-gun and cocked and recocked it angrily, then
remembered Hinch. The kid had faced Hinch—and won.

He lifted down a Winchester from the rack in the office
and went out late in the evening and knelt down behind a
water trough at the end of the street. Reb would come this
way when he made his last rounds.

It was dark when Reb finally appeared, coming from between buildings, walking slowly. There was a cold wind
blowing along the street, lifting dust to powder the air. The
only street lanterns were a block away in front of the bank.

HB laid the rifle across the trough and blinked to clear his
eyes; he sighted on Reb, swearing under his breath because
the kid stopped now and then and once disappeared entirely
to reappear suddenly in front of the photographer's shop. The
light was bad, but HB squeezed the trigger.

With the shot, Reb fell flat.

HB blinked rapidly. Had he hit the son of a bitch? He could
see nothing. The shop was perhaps fifty yards distant and
nothing moved there. He levered another shell into the chamber and got up, moving into the street.

Then, in a moment, he heard a calm voice from his right.
"Put the gun down, HB."

Turning his head, HB saw the kid, standing at the edge of
the street, a revolver in his hand. The kid cocked it, *click-
clack*. He said again, "Put the gun down."

HB hesitated. Hinch had been a gunfighter with a reputation—and this kid had beaten him. He would have to swing
around to his right to fire.

Sighing deeply, he laid the rifle on the ground and lifted
his arms.

Reb said, "The pistol, too. On the ground."

"You're a dead man," HB said. But gingerly he laid the
revolver beside the Winchester. He was boiling inside and
tried not to show it. He stepped into the street as Reb motioned toward the jailhouse. He watched the kid pick up the
two weapons and he suddenly lashed out. He was only a few
feet from the kid, but his fist did not connect as Reb evaded
it and pulled the trigger. The bullet almost grazed HB's cheek
and he wilted.

Reb said evenly, "The next one goes into you."

He put HB into a cell and locked the door, ignoring the
deputy's yells that he wanted a candle, he was in the goddamn dark!

Bushwhackers deserved very little in Reb's estimation.

The sheriff, Thomas Isher, arrived on the stagecoach,
astonished to learn Reb had the deputy in a cell. Isher was a
big, paunchy man with a gray mustache and rumpled clothes.
He sat in the office and listened to Reb's account as he smoked
a cigar.

He said, "They bring the horses here and HB sells 'em?"

"That's what I figure. HB probably has the contacts, the
actual thieves know where to get horses."

Isher nodded. "You never seen the others?"

"No. I saw some strangers, men who bought the horses,
that's all. I saw money exchanged."

"Umm." Isher leaned back. "How old you, son?"

"Twenty."

"Without us having the Bar H-O horses as evidence, it's
your word agin HB's."

"Yes. But let's check his bank account."

"I will."

"And one more thing . . . he tried to kill me."

Sheriff Isher talked to HB in his cell. HB denied selling stolen horses. There had been one Bar H-O horse in a bunch he'd received in a sale, but he had notified the buyer at once. If there had been another Bar H-O horse, he hadn't noticed it.

Isher dumped ashes on the floor. "Why'd you try to dry-gulch the kid?"

HB had no answer for that question. He remained in the cell.

Isher said to Reb, "Until the circuit judge gets here, you're the deputy. I'll be back for the trial."

Reb's pay was increased slightly and he saved some of it. But working for someone else was not his idea of a good job. He longed to be his own boss, and he thought continually about the freighting business. Why couldn't he start small and grow with it? All he'd need would be a wagon and team—and a lot of sitting on the seat traveling here and there.

But there was always the chance of a government contract one day . . . like Dustin's. It cost nothing to dream.

The circuit judge arrived in a specially constructed light spring wagon; it had a top and sides and a padded seat inside that could be folded back to make a bed. His assistant drove the team.

The assistant was also the clerk. He arranged to use the small ballroom of the Horseshoe Saloon as a courtroom and had several tables and chairs brought in. Chairs from the saloon were carried in for the audience.

The judge's name was Babcock. He was a big broad-shouldered man elegantly dressed. He wore a flowered vest and spectacles with a black ribbon attached. He came into the hushed room carrying a folder of papers and a small mallet. He seated himself at the desk and glanced at the people in the room with hard eyes.

The clerk said in a droning voice, "Hear ye, hear ye, the circuit court of the county of Inez is now in session, the honorable Alphonse Babcock presiding.'' He consulted with the judge a moment, shuffling papers. There were a number of small matters pending and the judge decided to tackle them first. He did not get to Deputy Bennett until after lunch.

HB was brought in with hands tied behind him, led by Sheriff Isher, with Reb behind. Isher untied his hands and pointed to a chair.

HB was then sworn in and promised to tell the truth. There were no attorneys present, there not being one within fifty miles.

At the judge's question HB denied selling stolen horses. He did not know about the Bar H-O horses.

''Don't you read the fliers that come into your office?''

''Yes, sir, but there are so many. . . . It's hard to remember them all.''

''Let me ask you one important question,'' the judge said. ''If you are not guilty of this crime, why did you attempt to kill your aide, Mr. Wiley?''

HB stammered and stumbled over words. The judge did not hurry him, but sat expectantly, brows raised. At length he said, ''Yes, Mr. Bennett?''

HB had no answer.

Sheriff Isher testified that he had investigated the deputy's bank account and found it to be two thousand, thirty seven dollars. No one in town had that much.

HB was found guilty.

It was the last case of the day and the judge cleared the room. HB's hands were tied again and the judge asked other questions concerning his partners in crime, their names, and where they could be found. HB's sentence would depend on his replies.

Ultimately he was sentenced to seven years in the territorial prison.

Reb was a full-fledged deputy sheriff, but the job was not to his liking. There was no challenge or satisfaction in locking up drunks. The few cases of petty crime hardly interested him. In one a man was accused of stealing chickens from a pen. The victim told Reb where to find the thief, and when Reb went to the man's shack and opened the door, he found the other cowering in a corner whimpering, ''Don't shoot me—don't shoot me—''

His reputation had gone ahead.

He quit the job when he had two hundred dollars saved.

He did not care much for the town of Gainesville and decided to move on. Then, in the weekly, he noticed Bert Wayland's name in the obituary column. With a certain amount of shock he read that Bert had died of natural causes . . . whatever that meant. He left only his wife, Marian.

Reb saddled up and rode to Haverford.

It was spring, an especially bad time to die. Wildflowers were out, brightening the fields and hills. Even the dowdy little town of Haverford seemed somehow refreshed as he rode in. And best of all, no one seemed to recognize him; he noticed no stares or people pointing.

He got down in front of the Wayland house and Marian came out onto the porch to greet him. She had been sitting by an open window and had seen him approach. They embraced on the steps and she cried softly on his shoulder, happy that he had come.

They went inside and she made tea for them. Bert had been buried three days past, she said, and the gravestone had not yet been put in place.

He asked, ''What will you do now?''

She had few friends in Haverford, she said, no one she would miss very much. ''I have an agent who will sell the feed barn and the house, and I'll go back to St. Louis, where I have kinfolks.''

Reb encouraged her in that. There was nothing here for her but memories.

When he left, he rode to the cemetery just outside the town on the slope of a gentle hill. Bert's was the only new grave.

Reb got down and walked to it and sat by the fresh mound as the light gradually left the hill.

He mounted the bay horse in the dusk and rode back to town slowly.

10

The sprawling town of Cooper was only twenty miles from Haverford. It was a bustling place because of the railroad spur and a stage-line depot and yard. The town already had a freighting company, an operation run by J. P. Drago. His name was on the wagons.

Reb hung around the depot and the railroad siding, watching the loading and unloading. Drago wagons backed up to the cars along with farm wagons and buckboards. He stopped by the Drago buildings and a clerk gave him a printed sheet explaining their charges and routes. Evidently Drago wagons hauled anywhere in the territory.

When Reb asked about Drago in the saloons, he got varying answers. Drago had a monopoly and many who had used his services were dissatisfied with him, usually because he took forever to deliver what was promiscd.

Reb then made the trip to the cattle ranch where Tim Foley kept accounts. He explained to Tim what he had in mind and asked Tim to partner with him in the venture.

"You stay in Cooper and I'll drive the wagon. We can sure make our beans, and we might do pretty good."

"What about Drago? He won't approve."

"Leave Drago to me."

Tim thought it over and finally agreed. He had a hundred dollars saved to put into the pot. He gave notice to an unhappy ranch boss and rode out with Reb.

In Cooper they rented a small barn off the main street. Reb hired a carpenter to tack on a room at the back for living quarters and, while that was being built, bought a wagon, a span of mules, and a Winchester rifle.

Tim talked a rancher into their first cargo; they met in a nearby saloon and the rancher was delighted to hear there was another outfit besides Drago's. His wife had ordered a pile of Eastern furniture, picked out of a catalog, and was nagging him for it.

Reb and Tim loaded it onto the wagon and delivered it the next day.

Reb brought back windmill parts to be repaired by the town blacksmith, so he had a load each way. They ought to make an effort to do that every time, Tim said. It was no good having a wagon and team return empty.

The next delivery was to Haverford, and Reb returned from that with a load of iron stoves from one merchant to another.

Reb got a night's sleep before he left on the wagon for Lyman, a town south of Cooper. He had a load of tanned leather and some kegs of mule shoes consigned to a blacksmith.

He returned with a load of produce.

And on the way back, met two horsemen.

They blocked the road. Both had rifles across their knees. One was skinny, the other burly and black-haired. The skinny one levered the Winchester.

Reb stood up in the wagon, opening his coat. "What you want?"

"We don't want nothin'," Skinny said. "But them mules look peaked as hell. Ought t'be put out of they misery." He was sallow faced and pockmarked. He extended the rifle and shot the near mule.

As it fell, flopping onto the road, Reb put two bullets into the man, flinging him off the horse. He turned the .44 to the second man, who instantly jerked his hands up.

Reb growled. "Who sent you?"

The man hesitated and Reb fired, cutting the brim of his hat as the man grabbed at it. He yelled, "Drago!"

Reb said, "Get down. Put 'im over the saddle and take him into town."

Black Hair got down slowly and wrestled the body up onto the saddle so it hung over each side.

Reb commandeered all the hardware, two rifles and two pistols, and dropped them into the wagon. They were probably five miles from town and Blackie would have to walk the horses.

He cut the dead mule out of the traces and moved on, reaching the town well ahead of them. He halted in front of the town marshal's office and went inside. The marshal was an old-timer, leathery and weather-wrinkled, named Jeff Larkin. He listened intently as Reb described what had occurred on the road and that Blackie had declared they were sent by Drago.

"You say he was a slim feller with pockmarks?"

"Yes."

Larkin nodded. "Think I know 'im then. Name of Targ. He's a hard case from down Texas way. Drago must have hired them both to take care o' you, you cuttin' into his business and all."

"There's enough for both of us."

The older man smiled. "He won't see it thataway."

Larkin went out and took charge of the weapons in the wagon. "I figger they won't be facing you next time they try something, Reb. So you watch your back."

"I will, Marshal, thanks."

Tim Foley was troubled when he heard what had happened. "They were going to shoot the mules and maybe you, too!"

"Yeah, maybe they had it in mind. . . ."

The local weekly *Clarion* printed the story. The gunfighter Reb Wiley had killed another man over a mule. The item was slanted in the dead man's favor and did not mention Drago. Reb read it and shook his head disgustedly.

He was so annoyed he called on the editor in his upstairs office. The door was open, so he went in and sat down opposite the man behind the desk. The other looked at him in surprise and took off his glasses. "Yes?" He was a middle-aged man with a square face and tight curly hair. He was in shirt sleeves with suspenders.

Reb said, "You printed a story about me that wasn't exactly true. My name's Reb Wiley."

The editor's eyes widened. "And so you came here to shoot me, too?"

Reb smiled. "Not at all. But I'm curious why you didn't tell what happened."

"We heard what happened from Mr. Ulrich. We assumed it was the truth."

"Who is Ulrich?"

"Ulrich and Targ were the two men you met on the road. You shot Targ—isn't that so?"

Reb nodded. "Because he shot my mule and would have shot me."

"Ulrich says it was an accident, that you ordered them off the road, shots were exchanged, and the mule was hit."

"None of that is true. Targ would have shot me and both my mules. *He* was the gunfighter, not me."

The editor's brows rose. "After all the gunfights you've been in?"

"Nearly every one was pushed onto me—just as this one was. It's my belief the two men were sent by Drago as part of his plan to drive me out of the freighting business."

"But you're the man who fought Peter Hinch!"

"He came after me. I didn't even know who he was."

"But you faced him down and killed him."

Reb shrugged. "I had to defend myself, sir."

The editor stared at him a moment. Then he leaned back. "So tell me your side of the story. . . ."

He considered going to call on Drago himself, though Tim was against it. "You'll end up shooting somebody—or getting shot. There may be ten to your one in that place. And what will you accomplish?"

"I'd ask him to stop annoying us."

Tim shook his head. "Useless." He changed the subject. "We need another mule."

There were no other incidents for more than three weeks. Tim had fliers printed and distributed, and their business grew to the point where another wagon and driver was necessary. The train brought in boxcars full of merchandise, all of which had to be delivered.

Reb bought another wagon and team, and Tim hired a young man, José Rivas. Tim was putting money in the bank, building their account.

Then one night their barn burned to the ground.

Reb was in Lyman with a load when it happened. Tim had been working late on accounts and had managed to get their important papers out. The barn was a total loss.

When he came into town and saw what had occurred, Reb rode at once to the Drago offices with a full head of steam. Tim yelled at him, but Reb pushed him aside.

The Drago company had a wide yard and several buildings. Reb rode in and jumped down, striding to the office, slamming the door open. A man blocked his way and Reb picked him up and tossed him through the door. He was in a square office, empty of people. Another door stood open and he hurried through it. Someone fired at him, emptying a pistol. All the shots went wild, most going into the walls and ceiling.

The .44 came out and he fired back, smashing a window. Men were yelling in the yard and he turned that way to see them scatter.

He went through the buildings, looking for Drago, and did not find him. Everyone scattered before him. He saw some of them running across the street.

He returned to Drago's office—there was a name on the door—and dumped the desk over, tossing papers everywhere. The clock struck three and he turned and put a bullet through it. Then he tossed a chair through the near window and went out to his horse . . . feeling much better.

* * *

Tim rented another building, across the street from the burned barn, and Marshal Larkin came to see them. Reb met him alone in the office.

Larkin said, "You really made a mess o' things, Reb."

"I intended to."

Larkin chuckled. "Drago wants you in jail a'course. But I figger there's enough suspicion against him about your barn that I won't do it. He hasn't lost anything much, 'cept his papers is ever' whichaway and he lost a good clock. What'd you shoot his clock for?"

Reb grinned. "I was mad as hell. Did you find out who set the fire?"

"Nobody knows anything. I guess it set itself. Kerosene walked over there and splashed itself all over the walls. We found the can, but it ain't talkin'."

"Do you know Drago?"

"I met him a few times, why?"

"Is he going to stop fighting us?"

Larkin fished out a cheroot and looked at it critically. "You want the truth—I doubt it. He's a hardheaded picker and I doubt if anybody can pound sense into him. He'll do 'er his way come hell or high water."

"He got out of his office when I went looking for him."

"He's hardheaded, but I didn't say he was stupid." Larkin struck a match. "He knows how good you are with that shootin' iron. But you've bucked him and he thinks this is his range." He lit the cheroot and puffed. "It ain't gonna occur to him that he's wrong."

11

The building they were in was small, but it had an apartment behind the offices, big enough for both of them, and a stable that they immediately enlarged. Their business went on almost without a halt.

In the next month Tim bought another team and wagon and hired two more drivers. Reb decided not to drive; he rode the bay with a Winchester across his thighs, acting as guard. There had been occasional altercations with Drago's drivers and loaders at the depot; however, when Reb showed up they stopped.

But he could not be everywhere.

José Rivas's wagon was attacked, miles from Cooper. Both mules were shot and killed. José slid off the seat and jumped into the willows and got away. But the attackers burned the wagon and cargo. Nothing was left.

José walked into town to report the loss.

When Reb heard about it, he rode to Drago's freight yard in a rage. The clerks ran out when they saw him coming. He upturned all the desks and smashed everything he touched. He did the same with Drago's office, turning it into a shambles, throwing chairs through all the windows.

When he went outside, a man came from the stable with a shotgun. Reb lifted the .44 and the man suddenly dropped the gun and ran.

He turned all the animals out of the stable, driving them into the street, then mounted the bay and stampeded them out of town.

* * *

When Marshal Larkin came to the office, he grinned on seeing Reb. "You got mad again, boy?"

"One of my men was nearly shot, the mules killed, and the wagon and everything in it destroyed."

"But how can you be sure it was Drago?"

"If the goods had been stolen instead of burned up, I might have thought something else."

"I see."

"It was a valuable cargo, which we had to pay for. I suspect Drago knew what it was. It's left us about flat broke. So the next time it happens I'm going after Drago himself. I wouldn't mind if you'd tell him that."

Larkin nodded. "An eye for an eye."

"Something like that."

Larkin talked to José about the attack and took his leave. And for a month there was no further trouble.

Then, according to the weekly, J. P. Drago was taken ill and went east to a hospital.

In a short while his son appeared and announced he was running the business until his father recovered. The son's name was Harvey Drago; he was twenty-two, unmarried, and had lived in the East most of his life.

He had been in Cooper less than two weeks when word came that his father had died.

At first there was no change. The truce that had existed for more than a month continued. Reb and Tim were hauling to Lyman once or twice a week, returning each time with produce that was sold locally. They began to build up their bank account again.

Then suddenly the Drago Company cut its rates in half.

They sent out advertising pieces with the new charges, took large space in the weekly, and in a very short time had all the freight business in the territory.

Reb and Tim could not compete.

It was necessary to lay off the drivers, sell the teams and

wagons, and go out of business. Tim hung a shingle in town and began to do accounting for various merchants.

Marshal Larkin offered Reb a job as deputy, and he accepted after a week of debate with himself. He had not yet come to terms with himself about what he wanted to do with his life. He had thought he wanted to be in business, to work for himself, but he had failed, because he hadn't the resources. The Drago Company had certainly lost money by cutting its rates, but it could afford to.

He did not want to be a lawman, but it was the path of least resistance. He was young and was gaining life experiences.

He turned twenty-two the week he went to work for Larkin.

Marshal Larkin was having problems with the two Welke brothers . . . when they came to town, which was about once every ten days. They were big, burly, dark men who were accustomed to using force for their needs. Few stood up to them. Those who did usually regretted it.

They liked the sound of breaking glass. When they got liquored up they loved to shoot out windows along the street. Of course the merchants were fed up with them, demanding that Larkin put a stop to the depredations.

That was not easy. Usually the two brothers came from a saloon late and shot out the windows as they galloped out of town.

If Larkin rode out to the Welke ranch alone, he would probably not come back.

The merchants figured the brothers owed them about two hundred dollars for glass and other breakage. They sent the brothers a bill, which was ignored.

In his office with Reb, Larkin said, "I figger the only way is to get the drop on them when they come into town—before they gets likkered up and mean. What you think?"

"It sounds good to me."

* * *

They put the plan into operation the next time the Welke brothers came to town and swaggered into the Cheyenne Saloon.

Larkin followed them in and, when they were standing at the bar, asked them in a loud voice to pay the two hundred dollars.

The brothers, Ham and Bud, turned in surprise and grinned, seeing him alone. "Well, hello, Marshal," Bud said. "What two hunnerd was that?"

"The town figgers you owe them that much." Larkin motioned. "You can put it on the bar behind you."

Ham growled. "You got a big mouth, Marshal. Whyn't you git the hell outta here?"

"I'm disappointed in you boys," Larkin said. "I thought you'd have more of a community spirit." He snapped at them. "Put the goddamn money on the bar!"

Both Ham and Bud grabbed at their hardware—and stopped short as a shot spanged into the ceiling. They both looked around in astonishment.

Reb stood a dozen feet to their right with a cocked pistol in each hand pointed at them.

Bud said, "Who the hell're you?"

Larkin said, "His name's Reb Wiley. He's my deputy. Put the money on the bar."

The two looked at each other and hesitated. Reb fired again, twitching Ham's hat. He pulled it off and stared at the hole. "Jesus!" They quickly complied, piling the money and stepping away as Larkin motioned.

As they left the saloon Bud said, "You ain't heard the last o' this, Marshal."

Larkin shrugged. "Don't get yourself dead over two hunnerd dollars, Bud."

Reb looked after them. "Folks say they're backshooters, Jeff."

Larkin nodded. "And folks're right. They're a couple of mean sons of bitches, and Bud's right, too. We haven't heard the last of it."

* * *

Nothing happened for a week. Then one night a rifle bullet splintered a livery-stable door as Larkin passed it on one of his rounds. He ran across the street in the direction from which it had come, but could locate no one.

"Probably one of the Welkes," he said to Reb in the office. "A hasty shot in poor light."

Neither of the brothers came into town for a month. Larkin said he'd heard they were going to Lyman for their flings. "It's just as well."

During this period Reb had written home several times, letting his father know where he was and that he was well. Todd always answered promptly and in his last letter mentioned that Isham was doing poorly. He had lost considerable weight and was often too weak to get out of bed.

The letter suggested that Reb come home. It did not say "if you want to see your uncle alive again," but Todd hinted at it.

Reb showed the letter to Larkin, rolled his blankets, and set out for Rustin.

Reb arrived in the middle of the night, put his horse in the stable, and went to sleep in the adjoining stall till daylight. When he saw his father was stirring in the house, he went inside to a delighted greeting.

Uncle Isham was still sleeping when he looked in on the older man. Reb was dismayed to see how gaunt he was.

"The doctor has seen him of course."

"Yes, many times. He says it's an internal cancer. There's nothing anyone can do."

"Does Isham know?"

"Yes, he knows." Todd sighed deeply. "The doctor gives him only a few months. . . ."

Reb went into town to see Albe Newlan and Henry Jorganson. Albe seemed not a day older, but Henry was more lined and getting a little stooped. Both men made a fuss over him and Henry insisted on buying him a drink.

There were great changes at the fort, Henry said when they stood in the saloon with their feet on the brass rail. Most

72   Arthur Moore

of the men had been shipped away; there was only a skeleton housekeeping force there now.

"The talk is," Henry said, "the army is goin' to sell the whole lot. They don't need it no longer."

"Sell the fort?"

"They got a bigger installation at Fort Taylor. It's just a hunnerd miles down the road. They don't need two."

"That's going to cut into the town's business."

"It has already. I bet you Albe ain't sold five bottles of whiskey this month. You lookin' bigger each time we see you, Reb."

"I'm fine."

"I see you still got that old .44 Isham gave you."

"I'm used to it."

He had a young deputy, Henry told Reb, and was thinking of retiring. "M'wife wants to go south to her folks' place in Alabama. And we might do 'er come summer. How you like bein' a lawman?"

"It's a living," Reb confessed, "I'd like to find something better, though."

"Hell, there's lots of things better, but most of 'em requires schoolin'. I never could get past that . . . but you can."

Reb chuckled. "I was never much good at school—always looking out the window."

"You ever hear from Lem Cotter?"

"No, not a word. I guess he's made a life for himself and forgot about us out here in the sticks."

"I guess so."

Isham died a month before they were prepared for the death. Todd entered the room one morning to find him cold. He had died in the night.

If he had to go, Todd said, that was the way to do it.

The undertaker, Mr. Frobisher, came for the body, and the funeral was held several days later. Twenty-five or thirty people attended the graveside service and Reb rode home with his father in the old black buggy, feeling his childhood was long behind him. Isham had been so bound up with those early years. . . .

Reb stayed for a week after the funeral. His father seemed unable to accept that Isham was gone. He talked of him continually and even spoke often as if Isham were in the next room. The two men had shared the house since Leona had died, and now Todd had no one—except Reb.

He talked of opening the house to boarders. Or even of selling the house and going to live in a boardinghouse, where there would be others around, his own age.

He was still talking about it when Reb left.

On returning to Cooper, Reb found Marshal Jeff Larkin at home with his shoulder all bound up in bandages. He lived in a boardinghouse and the doctor had been to see him every day and he was drinking laudanum.

A bullet had taken the top of his shoulder off. It had gone in the back and the bone was shattered.

"It took half the bone with it," Larkin said disgustedly. "The doc ain't sure if I'll ever use the arm again."

"Who shot you?"

"One of the Welkes. I think it was Bud."

"How'd they get behind you?"

"I walked past 'em on the street at night and didn't see 'em. They was hiding behind some boards. I was just lucky they didn't finish me. I figger they thought I was dead, so they skedaddled."

"Did you see them to be sure?"

Larkin nodded. "When I fell, I seen Bud—grinnin' at me."

It had happened a week after Reb had left to go to Rustin, and the Welkes had been seen in town one time after the shooting, making jokes about the marshal.

It was too much for Reb. He rode out to the Welke ranch, arriving after dark. Jeff Larkin was hurt bad and might have a useless arm the rest of his life. He was going to see that the Welkes were a little uncomfortable, too—as a starter.

He left the bay horse in a draw and walked to the ranch house. It was little more than a large shack, a one-story affair, unpainted and as rough as the two brothers themselves. There were lights inside, but only a few windows had glass. Most were boarded up or had blankets tacked across them.

Behind the shack, maybe a hundred yards away, was the bunkhouse. It looked better built, a long building with two tin chimneys and a corral at one end. Near the corral was a barn and some sheds.

He waited till the lights in the house went out, then he piled up weeds along the side of the house, chest-high. When he struck a match and lighted it, the bone-dry weeds flared up in seconds.

Reb stepped away from the shack, watching the boards catch as the flames ate at the wood greedily. When it was going good, too good to put out, he drew the Colt and fired four shots at the iron chimney. The shots would wake the Welkes in time to get out.

He got on the bay and rode back to town. The shack was a goner and now the Welkes would be a little more uncomfortable. They would lose everything in the house, clothes, tally books, everything. But not as much as Larkin.

The following day the two Welkes came roaring into town, loaded for bear. They galloped to the jail office, yelling for Larkin. Each man carried a shotgun.

Reb had expected some such show and was across the street, waiting for them. Larkin was in the office, bundled up, white and drawn.

When the brothers shouted for Larkin to come out, Reb moved into the street. "You're probably looking for me."

The two whirled around, staring at him. For an instant they were silent—maybe recalling what had happened in the saloon when they'd been forced to pay over the money.

"It's him!" Bud said, through clenched teeth. Then he grinned. They were two to his one this time.

"Ride on out," Reb said, "and nobody gets hurt."

Instead, Ham yanked the shotgun around to shoot. Reb's .44 was in his hand and spit fire. Ham was knocked from the saddle. The shotgun fired into the air and clattered to the street. All in a second.

Bud Welke stared into the muzzle of the Colt.

He got down slowly and knelt by the body of his brother. "He's dead!" He glowered at Reb. "You kilt him, you sombitch!"

"He was stupid," Reb said evenly. "You got a choice, are you stupid, too?"

Bud growled under his breath.

Reb said, "Get out of town."

"He got to go to the undertaker's."

"All right. Then take him." Reb watched Bud hoist the body onto the nervous horse, glaring at Reb. Then he walked, leading both horses, paying no attention to the gawkers who lined the walks.

Larkin came from the office and leaned on the side of the building, looking after Bud. "You got one rattler, Reb, but there's still one to go."

Reb nodded slowly. He could not have shot Bud down, but he knew he would regret it one day.

Reb did not attend the funeral for Ham Welke, but neither did anyone else in the town. Bud was the sole mourner; he got very drunk in a saloon afterward and managed to climb onto his horse and ride back to the ranch, muttering to himself.

He did not contract with anyone in town to rebuild the ranch house and was apparently living in the bunkhouse.

Jeff Larkin's wound caused him endless pain, despite the laudanum. He had no end of trouble sleeping. It was impossible, he said, to find a comfortable place. He could no longer function as Marshal, and the job passed to Reb.

A month after the shooting he decided to travel to Kansas

City, to be examined by doctors there, in hopes of some improvement.

Reb saw him off on the stagecoach, and as the rig rattled out of town a buckboard appeared, coming in the opposite direction, driven by Bud Welke.

12

Welke stared straight ahead, paying no attention to anyone on the street. He stopped the wagon in front of the general store and went inside with a list.

When he came out, it was to pile several boxes and sacks in the wagon bed. Then he drove on, stopping at the black-smith's and one other store and the Trail's End Saloon. He remained in the saloon for three hours, leaving just before dark to drive back to the ranch.

Reb watched him out of town.

The next time he appeared in the town, Bud put the ranch up for sale.

At the end of a month a letter came to Reb from Kansas City. Larkin wrote that a famous surgeon had agreed to operate on him, and he was sure it would make a great difference for good. He expected to have use of his arm and shoulder, even though it would be somewhat limited. He would be coming home as soon as the doctor said he could travel.

It was three weeks before he arrived and a dozen people were at the depot when Larkin, with help, got off the train, smiling broadly. His arm was still in a sling and he looked very thin and wan. Reb helped him into the buggy he'd brought and he waved to everyone, exchanging greetings.

But he was through as a lawman, thanks to Welke. His arm would never be the same, he told Reb. The surgeon had done a fine job, but he was not God; he could do only so much. Larkin could dress himself perfectly well, but he had limited strength in his hand. Welke had done for him very effectively.

He came to the office each day and sat at his old desk. There was much he could do. He had a term to serve out, after all.

It was good that Cooper was a quiet town; the merchants could not afford a third lawman. Reb easily kept order, Larkin did the paperwork, and matters seemed to be settled.

Until Larkin was shot again as he left the office one night. This time the shot came from behind and sliced just under his ribs on the right side. Larkin fell in the grass and lay perfectly still, playing dead. With his ear close to the ground he could hear the drumming of hoofbeats as the assassin galloped away into the dark.

Several people, having heard the shot, came out and found him there. One ran for the doc and another for Reb. They carried Larkin inside, and when Doc Weiss came, he treated and dressed the wound.

"It's a flesh wound, not serious," he told Reb. "Not life threatening at all. Whoever shot him missed by about four inches of doing great harm. It'll irritate him like bloody hell, but I'll give him some laudanum for pain." Weiss shook his head. "These shootings are really more than he needs."

It had to be Welke, Reb thought. A parting shot.

He rolled his blankets, tied on some airtights, and took out for the Welke ranch that same night.

He did not expect Welke to be at the ranch, and he was not. The ranch shack had not been rebuilt. There were two riders in the bunkhouse and they said they had not seen Bud Welke for several days. The ranch had been sold and Welke had no business there now anyway.

Reb asked, "Where is Welke likely to go?"

"South," they both said at once. "He always talked about going back south. He came from a town called Lamond."

Neither of them had ever heard of it.

Lamond. It was not on any map he'd seen. It was probably some little one-horse burg in the middle of nowhere.

Reb headed south, looking for tracks, and found none.

He had no worries about leaving Cooper behind. Larkin would hire an assistant. He was far more concerned with finding the man who had shot Larkin twice. And he was the only one who could go after Welke.

In a dusty little trading post he heard tidings of Welke. When Reb described him, the owner said such a man had been there the day before, riding a roan horse. He had gone on south and east.

Two days later in a windy small town he missed Welke by what was probably minutes. He later realized he must have gone in the front door of the hotel while Welke went out the back. The other probably knew he was being followed. Now Reb would have be careful of an ambush.

It slowed him up. Reb rode with the butt of the Winchester resting on his thigh, the hammer back, ready to fire. He scanned the trail ahead with binoculars and rode around suspicious outcroppings. Now and then he found places where someone had waited, and twice he drew shots that were probably aimed at his bay horse.

Welke was apparently not a good marksman. He had not been able to kill Larkin in two different attempts. Maybe he got excited and jerked the trigger. . . .

One afternoon a light rain swept over him, and when it passed, he found tracks—that led him into Lamond.

It was a larger town than Cooper, of brick and clapboard buildings. There was a railroad, stock pens along a siding, and stockyards behind. A stagecoach came clattering into town just before him, halting with a squealing of brake blocks and double-tree chains; passengers climbed down wearily and went into a large front-flared building.

Reb signed for a room in the Lamond Hotel and learned the town was named after a senator who had served before the war. He did not inquire about Welke; if this were his hometown, there was no telling who might relay information to Welke. Reb signed as Jack Harris, from Amarillo. He had seen the name on a theater once.

That done, his horse in the stable, he stood on the street wondering where to start looking for Welke. The man might have gone through the town and was miles away by now.

He went upstairs to bed.

In the morning Reb went into the Alamo Saloon. Like it or not, there was only one way to learn about Welke. Ask questions. The only bartender had never heard the name. In the next saloon the barman shook his head.

In the third saloon, The Triangle, the bartender looked mildly surprised. "He sittin' right over there." He pointed and Reb turned.

Bud Welke was staring at him from a table in the center of the room. He was playing cards with two others. As Reb turned, Welke pulled a gun and started shooting.

Reb extended his arm with the .44 and fired twice. The shots knocked Welke backward out of the chair. He sprawled on the board floor, arms outflung. His pistol bumped away.

For a moment the saloon was hushed. Then everyone began chattering at once. Someone bent over Welke and shook his head.

Reb reloaded automatically. He was not touched by any of Welke's wild shots, several of which had smashed the backbar mirror and two others rapped into the bar near him. Welke had a double-action revolver and had fired five shots as fast as he could pull the trigger. They had all hit to Reb's right.

He watched two men carry the body out to the boardwalk, then he went back to the hotel. A deputy sheriff found him there an hour later.

"I got to put you under arrest, mister. . . . Lemme have your gun."

Reb handed it over and was taken to the local jailhouse. The deputy was a lanky, taciturn man who answered questions shortly or not at all. Reb was in jail because he had shot Welke. It was all the deputy would tell him.

He lay on the cot in jail for two weeks before his trial. Then the deputy tied his hands behind him and walked him to the courthouse, a shacky building with a makeshift kind of steeple atop it.

He was the fifth defendant to stand before the judge, Elmer Stoddard, a hard-faced man in his early sixties, who stared at him as the charge was read.

"How d'you plead, Wiley?"

"Self-defense, Your Honor." Nothing was said about an attorney to defend him.

"Self-defense?" Stoddard sounded as if he had never heard those words before.

"Welke pulled a gun and fired. I had to defend myself or be killed."

"Is that so . . ." The judge motioned. "Sit down."

A stout man in a wrinkled store suit was sworn in, gave his name as Herbert Toms, and the judge asked him to tell what he had seen in the saloon when the shooting took place.

"Yes, sir." The witness frowned at Reb. "Bud Welke was sitting at a table with Jim and Fred when this man"— he pointed to Reb—"came in and pulled his gun."

Reb said, "Only after Welke—"

The judge rapped hard with his gavel. "Quiet, dammit! Go on, Herb." He glared at Reb.

"That's it, Your Honor. This here man killed him."

Both Jim and Fred told the same story. Reb had come in and opened fire.

Reb protested that Welke had fired at him five times! But it did no good. He was sentenced to nine years in the territorial prison at Eversville.

The deputy took him back to the cell to await transportation.

Reb said, "Is that the kind of justice you have in this place?"

The deputy did not meet his eyes. "You shot the wrong man, Wiley."

"What's that mean?"

"You shot the judge's nephew."

13

The territorial prison sat on a flat plain with the south fork of the Bone River a quarter of a mile distant. A ditch had been dug to the river, so water flowed once a day into a huge well-like cistern. From the cistern water was piped into the prison.

Two convicts were sent each morning under guard to muscle the big iron wheel so water entered the ditch. They turned it off when a flag waved to show the cistern was full.

The other inmates worked in the fields where vegetables and other crops were grown; the eatables fed the prison populace. A few convicts who had had schooling worked in the prison offices. The prison was built somewhat in the manner of a Spanish presidio with a parade ground in the center and the offices, shops, cells, barracks, storerooms, and other rooms around it. The offices were beside the main gate, two stories high, thus overlooking the entire establishment.

Reb was put to work in the fields.

He heard varying stories. Some said that no one had ever escaped from the prison, some said that a few had made it. From the first day he looked for a chance. He had been railroaded and did not belong here.

He was put into a cell with a thief named Slate Lawler, a skinny, grinning man who seemed to know all about him. "We see papers now'n then. You shot Bud Welke."

"Did you know him?"

"Naw. We just heard about it." Slate laughed. "And him

83

and the judge was kinfolk. You shoulda got the rope. I'm surprised the judge didn't hang you right in the courtroom.''

The prisoners were marched in groups each morning to work in the fields. Each group of ten men had a mounted guard with pistol and rifle, watching over them.

Reb and Slate were put into one group and marched off under the direction of a burly guard the men called Bad Ass . . . to his back. He had a reputation as a man very quick on the trigger; it was said he had killed two inmates who had stepped out of line.

They were given equipment and told to hoe weeds in the rows. It was not required to be enthusiastic, the older hands told Reb, but it was necessary to work steadily, not to draw attention from Bad Ass. He was capable of hounding a man unmercifully.

He sat his horse a dozen yards away, behind them, watching and smoking a cigar. He allowed no one to come close and he followed along slowly as they worked the rows.

Bad Ass looked half-asleep, but when a man stepped from the row he'd been working on, the guard drew back the hammer of his rifle, *click-clack*. No word was spoken and the man jumped back again.

Slate said under his breath, ''Don't take no chances with him.''

Reb soon discovered there were a dozen different plans for escape circulating among the inmates. But they had no organization, probably because they did not trust each other. Everyone was wary of informers.

The first week he was in the prison, he wrote to Larkin, explaining the circumstances and details, telling the other where he was. According to the rules, inmates were allowed to send out one letter a month, after it was read by prison authorities. They could receive any number, but in practice it was seldom that anyone received anything.

''We never get an answer to nothing,'' Slate told Reb. ''I been writing letters since I got here two years ago. I never got an answer yet. I don't think they send out our letters.''

That would certainly keep complaints to a minimum, Reb thought. And the prison authorities could easily control that simply by dumping all outgoing mail in the fire.

However, they could not control the releases of men who had served their sentences. They could and did delay those releases by petty means, but not for too long. And those released men told about the unsatisfactory conditions at the prison. Newspapers gleefully printed them.

Reb gave a note to a man about to be released; it was three lines to Jeff Larkin and the man concealed it in his hat, knowing he would be searched. The searchers missed it and it was received in due time by Larkin—who was astonished. Reb in prison!

Reb had been gone a month when Larkin arrived in Lamond. There were two deputies in the town and he talked to one, as an ex-lawman himself, shot up in the line of duty. The shooting of Bud Welke was mentioned and Larkin learned the deputy did not agree with the findings of the court. The deputy thought the judge was prejudiced, that Wiley had been unjustly convicted. The judge should have disqualified himself.

"Besides," the deputy said, "Welke fired five times at Wiley in the saloon and missed ever' time. Wiley hit 'im twice in the ticker. That means that if Wiley had fired first like they said in court, then Welke would never have got off a single shot."

"The judge didn't allow that evidence?"

"He didn't allow none of it. Wiley was railroaded into jail."

The prison was forty miles south of Lamond near the little burg of the same name, Eversville. It was not really a town, only a store, a saloon, and a stage way station. Released prisoners were dropped off at the station and given a ticket.

Larkin got off the stage there and hired a horse and saddle from the storekeeper. He rode the few miles to the prison, to look it over. It had the appearance of a fort, mean and ugly, a dirty gray in color, squatting on the plain like a huge toad. It was surrounded by a barbed-wire fence and signs asked travelers and gawkers to keep their distance.

He could see workers in the fields near the prison and guards on horseback. Larkin spent more than an hour looking at the place and could see no way to break Reb out. Mostly because there was no way to communicate with an inmate. How could they make plans?

Letters never got through, the storekeeper told Larkin, and even if they did, it would take weeks, and besides, each letter was read. It was hopeless.

There was no place for him to stay in Eversville, so he took the next stage, feeling very discouraged. It did not seem there was anything at all he could do to help Reb.

The fields were extensive, stretching back nearly half a mile behind the prison buildings, all the way to the river.

Not all the inmates worked in the fields; some worked in the shops, the laundry, the bakery, some were in the infirmary, some in solitary. . . . There were about a hundred men in all, Slate told Reb. The easiest jobs were held by toadies.

But work in the fields was not especially hard. It was tiring because Bad Ass did not allow any rest periods. They were allowed half an hour at noon to eat the hardtack they were given and to drink water. At the end of the day they were exhausted.

As a result they slept like dead men from lights out to the morning whistle. Few felt like sitting up in the dark to plan escapes.

The prison sat on a level plain, but there were hills and mountains all around it. The nearest, to the north, looked to be about twenty miles away, Reb thought. If a man could reach those hills, he might lose a posse.

But to reach the hills, he'd have to ride a horse.

The prison had a stable housing a half-dozen horses and a couple of mules, two buggies, and a light wagon. But no inmates were used for stablework. Two employees drove the wagon into Eversville several times a week on various errands. Reb watched it go; he could see it as he worked at weeding. But there was no way to get close. And no way to get to the stable, which was outside the wall.

The only horse he got close to belonged to Bad Ass.

He mentioned that fact one night to Slate, who said, "He's a killer, Reb. You step out of line and he'll shoot. I seen him do it."

But Bad Ass was only a few feet away. If his attention were diverted for a moment—would that be enough? He'd have to pull the man off the horse and get hold of one of his guns at the same time. And he'd probably have to shoot to kill. Bad Ass would kill him in an instant—if he could.

When he discussed it with Slate late at night in their cell, Slate shivered and shook his head. If the attempt failed, Bad Ass would kill them both.

"He's a guard, Reb. He'll say we was tryin' to escape and that'll be the end of it. Except we'll be dead."

Reb stared at him.

Slate said, "And one more thing—nobody will help you. They afraid of gettin' shot, too."

"I think I can reach him."

"Nobody else has!"

"Has anybody tried it—that you know of?"

Slate sighed deeply. "Well, a couple has stepped out of line and Bad Ass shot 'em. I dunno if they was tryin' to reach him." Slate kept shaking his head. "It's too goddamn risky, Reb. He's too quick."

"But he's only a few feet away. I'll dump him off the horse, or pull him off."

"Then what'll you do? If any shots is fired, ever'body in the prison will turn out. They'll ring the damn bell—and you can hear it for miles. They'll be after you like heel flies!"

Reb mused. "That's a pretty good horse he's riding. I'd take that chance. What about you?"

Slate hunched narrow shoulders. "I'm not goin' nowhere. I'll git out in another two years—in one piece. If you do it, you go alone, Reb. Sorry."

* * *

Each day thereafter, Reb watched Bad Ass out of the corner of his eye, examining everything about the man, how he
sat the saddle, his toes usually barely in the stirrups. How he
held the Winchester, mostly across his heavy thighs, a finger
in the trigger guard. Bad Ass was a big, paunchy man with
a stomach that touched the saddle horn. He wore his flat-
brimmed hat close down over beady eyes and often appeared
half-asleep, but Reb noted that the rifle moved slightly any
time one of the workers happened to take a step outside one
of the plant rows. Bad Ass was alert.

He also wore a pistol holstered for a fast cross draw, but
he obviously depended on the rifle for an emergency; his
thumb rested on the hammer at all times, ready to yank it
back.

But he'd had no emergency, Slate said, for about two years.
He had shot a man then, but only wounded him. The inmate
had stumbled and fell as he was shot, and Bad Ass had only
spurred out of reach. He hadn't fired again.

''We was all surprised he didn't kill 'im,'' Slate said.

Reb wondered at that, too.

And then, by mere chance, as he was passing the prison
office windows, he caught sight of Bad Ass reading a paper,
and he was wearing what looked like thick glasses!

Glasses! The guard had never worn glasses on duty in the
fields. Did he have blurry vision? Was that why he hadn't
killed the inmate with a second shot? He had feared he'd
miss? Then everyone would know! Was Bad Ass half-blind?

14

Summer passed into fall and rains kept the field gangs indoors. But when the rains let up, weeds appeared and the men went out again.

Reb decided to make his break that fall—whenever it seemed a likely time. He no longer talked to Slate about breaking out, fearing the man would inform on him. If Slate knew he was going to make a break, he might talk to save his own skin.

So Reb pretended he'd given up the idea. But he watched Bad Ass as never before. And noticed that Bad Ass never consulted his watch as he once had. Now he depended on the prison bell to tell him when to form up the inmates and return. His eyes *were* bad.

Exactly how bad was impossible to tell. Reb decided to test the guard, and one afternoon he stepped away from the row he was weeding, and stepped back at once.

He expected Bad Ass would turn the rifle toward him, but the Winchester did not move.

Reb decided to make the break the next day.

He had been concealing food in his mattress for a week, hiding it from Slate. In the morning when the gang was called out, Reb put the food in his pockets and marched away to the fields with the others.

It was a brisk morning and he was keyed up, but doing his best not to show it. He had thought to make the break early, maybe even before the men had settled down to the routine.

Bad Ass might be less alert then. And the people in the prison might take much longer to get a pursuit organized.

As the work began and the men spread out in rows, chopping at the tall weeds, Reb moved to the outside, closest to Bad Ass, and picked up a handful of heavy round stones. He was perhaps fifteen feet from the guard when he hurled the first one. It hit the pommel of the saddle and Bad Ass jerked his head around, startled.

The second rock hit him in the neck and Reb was charging.

Coughing and choking, Bad Ass did not see him for a moment. Then Reb was on him, heaving the big man from the saddle like a sack of oats, grabbing the Winchester at the same time. Bad Ass hit the ground heavily. Reb swung up into the saddle, turned the horse, and kicked with his heels. The inmates were yelling as he galloped away.

Bad Ass managed to roll onto his stomach and fire six shots, but they all went wild.

Reb expected to hear the bell at the prison ring quickly, but it seemed to take a long while and he was miles away before it started to ring like a mad thing.

The plain was flat, studded with high brush and some piñon pine; after a few miles he could no longer see the prison buildings.

But he was leaving a plain trail that anyone could follow. He tried to stay in as straight a line as possible; that way he would cover the most ground. He would take evasive action later when he gained the hills.

He felt a high exhilaration—he was free! Of course he could never come back to this particular corner of the land or they would grab him—if they could. But he had been jailed by a biased judge and he did not feel like a lawbreaker.

The horse was a good animal. They might charge him with horse stealing and swiping the Winchester. Too bad. The rifle had a full magazine and one in the chamber. Carved on the stock were the initials HT. Probably Bad Ass's name—whatever it was.

By dusk he had not seen or heard a pursuit. He entered

the hills, winding his way in the dark, walking the horse. He would return to Cooper and discuss his future with Jeff Larkin. If someone from the prison showed up there, it ought to be easy to evade him. Of course they might expect him to go to Cooper. . . .

As he rode he ate what food he had. When the moon came out, icy and bright in a star-filled sky, he let the horse crop grass by a stream while he dozed.

He went on at first light.

It was a quiet afternoon in Cooper when Jeff Larkin opened the office stove and poked in more sticks. It had rained for an hour earlier, but now the sky was mottled and patches of blue were showing. A chilly wind was sweeping down the main street and folks were staying inside.

He glanced around as the door opened, then sat up and yelled, ''Reb!''

Reb grinned and shook hands with the other.

''You busted out of jail?''

Reb nodded. ''Had to. Nobody came to get me.''

''Well, damn my eyes! I thought you were a hopeless case. They had you railroaded for good.''

Reb held out his hands to the warmth of the stove. ''The judge and Welke were kinfolk. I got myself into a stacked deck.''

''I found that out when I went down there.''

''You went there?''

''Sure. To see what it was all about. Nobody gave you a chance. You hungry?''

''Starved.''

''Let's go get us some vittles.''

They got a corner table in the restaurant, away from everyone, and Reb explained how he had dumped Bad Ass off the horse and galloped off into the hills.

''Do you think they'll come after me?''

Larkin shrugged. ''They'll send out fliers, of course. But it depends on how mad the judge is, and how much money the treasury has to pay for a deputy to make the trip on suspicion alone. I kind of doubt it. If they knew where you were—for certain—they probably would.''

''They know I came from here.''

''Yes, but I think the biggest worry is a bounty hunter. If the flier says 'dead or alive,' then he might try to backshoot you.''

''Well, any description they give would fit a thousand men.''

Larkin smiled. ''If a deputy does show up, I'll get the local paper to print a story about how the judge and Welke were related. It might raise some stink.'' He frowned. ''Maybe I'll do it anyhow.''

Reb took up his job as deputy as if nothing had intervened; no one from Lamond made an appearance. The Eversville prison was hundreds of miles away and news did not percolate across the prairie with any speed. As Larkin said, they might never hear that Reb was working in Cooper.

And a month passed.

Then, despite all their assumptions, a man did show up at the jail office asking about Reb Wiley. He was a rough-looking character wearing a faded, patched duster and an old curl-brim hat. He had a tied-down holstered pistol and one of the fliers on Reb. He gave his name as Karg and said he was looking to collect the bounty.

Larkin glanced at the flier; it was the same as the one he'd received in the mail. He shook his head. ''Ain't seen him.''

''I unnerstand he worked for you.''

''Yeah, he did. Before he went to prison.''

As they were talking, Reb came into the office, nodding to the stranger. Larkin said quickly. ''This's Karg. He's lookin' for Reb Wiley. Where you figger he got to?''

''Hard to say,'' Reb said. ''He came from Rustin. Maybe he went back there.'' He kept his head turned away so the scarred side of his cheek was not visible.

''Rustin?'' Karg said. ''Izzat north of here?''

Larkin had a map pinned to the wall. He got up and located the town as Karg peered over his shoulder. Larkin said,

"You ought to have a picture of him. He might change his name."

"No picture available. Guess he never had one took. What did he look like when he worked for you?"

Larkin scratched his jaw. "Let's see. . . . He was taller'n me by a couple inches and a lot bigger man."

Reb asked, "Did you say he had a mustache?"

"Yeah, he had one, but he shaved it off . . . only I think he was growin' it again when he left here." He turned as Reb went into the jail area and closed the door.

Karg said, "Who was that?"

"My deputy, Henry."

"Ever'body's got a mustache," Karg said in a growling voice. "Well, most ever'body. Did he have anything like a limp or a tattoo?"

Larkin shook his head. "Nope."

"They told me he had a scar on his cheek."

"Well, if he did, you can't hardly see it. I don't even remember it."

"When was the last time you seen him?"

"Oh, maybe a few days before he went to that town where they grabbed him."

"Lamond."

"Was that it?" Larkin sat down by the stove. "Sorry I can't help you much. I do remember him talkin' about going to St. Louis though."

"Jesus—St. Louie?"

"Said he knew folks there."

Karg sighed deeply. "All right. Thanks, Mr. Larkin." He went out to his horse.

Reb came from the back cell area and they watched the man ride away, bending low in the wind. Larkin said, "Damn shame I couldn't help him collect his bounty."

"How much did he say?"

"He didn't say, but this here flier says four hunnerd. That's all you're worth—delivered to Eversville."

Reb grunted. "That's not much for a desperate man. They don't want me bad."

"Your friend Bad Ass does, I'm sure. He'd probably pay it out of his own pocket to get you back again."

Reb laughed. "And I wouldn't last ten minutes."

The Cooper County Bank stood proudly in the very center of town on a corner, a two-story red-brick building with high gingerbread cornices and gold leaf on the windows. It was owned by Martin Finerty, long a pillar of the community as his father had been; Martin was now approaching his seventy-first birthday.

He was working in his office with the door open; it was just off the main room of the bank. He saw the three robbers enter and pull up wipes to hide their faces. He sat in shock for half a minute until one ordered him out and into another room with the rest of the employees.

The robbers filled gray canvas sacks with money scooped up from the tellers' cages and from the open safe. They were efficient and said little among themselves, as if they had done this many times before.

Martin Finerty was enraged. The robbers were taking every penny he owned! He scrabbled in a desk drawer for a pistol and ran to the door, firing at the three as they headed for the street.

One turned and fired three times at Finerty—who was flung down. The robbers escaped.

Jeff Larkin happened to be across the street when he heard the shots fired. He ran out in time to see four men gallop their horses away from the bank. Larkin was unarmed and could only stare helplessly after them.

Then he hurried into the bank to find Martin Finerty dead.

Reb also heard the shots and jogged to the bank, where people were gathering. He pushed through and Larkin took him aside.

"It was the Collins gang. I recognized Hop Collins when he came out—he was probably the one who shot Finerty."

"They killed Finerty?"

"Yes. Unfortunately Marty tried to swap shots with them.

There were four in all, one held the horses out front. It was Hop and probably his brother, Ames, and two others.''

"I'll get a posse together.''

He collected five men besides himself and they rode out after the robbers in less than half an hour.

One of the five was a tracker named Shotgun Dawes; he had never told anyone his real name, so most suspected it was one of the curious ones that doting mothers bestowed on helpless children. Shotgun had been employed by the army for a good many years and Reb was glad to get him. He did not know the other men.

Shotgun was a wiry old-timer, not very garrulous and not at all respectful of authority, the reason the army had let him go. He rode a dozen or more yards in front of the posse, his eyes on the trail. Occasionally the first day he halted them and got down to walk a bit, stooped over, stopping, then going on and finally waving to them to come on.

When it got dark, they made camp. "Best lay over," he said to Reb.

It was an uncomfortable camp with no water nearby, and Reb was glad when dawn came poking over the far hills as if reluctantly.

They went on and Shotgun apparently had no trouble following the outlaw's trail. "They were more careless," he said to Reb, "the farther they got." Probably not expecting much of a pursuit.

However, they had another uncomfortable camp and the third day out two men decided they'd had enough. They were not prepared for a long trip, they said, and it was no skin off their asses if the bank lost money. They turned back.

The next morning, another man was missing; he had packed up during the night.

Reb considered. They were now three in all—the robbers outnumbered them. Should they go on? He put it to a vote. The third man was a young rider from a neighboring ranch. His name was Tate Ransom and he voted with Reb to go on. Shotgun declared it didn't matter to him one way or another. Tate was interested in the reward, he told them. One had not been announced from the bank before they rode out.

"But they got to be a reward," Tate said. "If my split is enough, I going to send for a girl from St. Louis."

"A particular girl?" Reb asked.

"Her name's Ellie. She said she'd marry me."

Shotgun snorted. "Marry—"

Reb looked at him. "You were married once?"

"Yeh, once. She run off with a gambler." Shotgun glared at the younger man. "Wimmin is no damn good."

Tate frowned, then glanced at Reb and his face cleared.

Reb said, "Let's get moving."

15

Shotgun proved to be a difficult man to get along with, though an excellent tracker. He had spent much of his life alone, out in the sticks, and he was unused to sharing anything, especially the night watches. He was sure, he said, that if anyone tried to slip up on them during the night, he would hear them.

Reb voiced his objections, but Shotgun snarled and growled, refusing to take a watch, declaring the robbers were intent on putting distance between them. ''You kin see the way they hustlin' along.''

The trail led to the ragged collection of shacks that called itself Arkwright. It had a main street only a hundred yards long, with half a dozen weather-beaten clapboard buildings with brave false fronts, all faded.

Yes, four men had come into town, Reb was told, and had gone out again after buying a few staples at the store. They had come into town the day before and left within an hour or two, pointing south.

The road south, they were told, between Arkwright and Pinal, was well traveled and Shotgun lost the tracks in soft dust. They rode all the way to Pinal, a burg the size of Arkwright, to learn that four men together had not reached there.

''Damn! They done turned off some'eres,'' Shotgun said disgustedly.

It was necessary to go back, watching both sides of the road for signs, which made travel very slow. They came on a number of likely tracks before Shotgun discovered the real trail, which led south and east. The robbers had gone around Pinal.

"They headin' for Maples," Shotgun declared. "It's the biggest town in these parts."

Tate agreed, and they were probably right, Reb mused.

The four were about two days ahead of them and the trail was getting cold. Shotgun strongly suggested they forget the tracking and go directly to Maples.

Tate was of the same opinion. "We'll find 'em there."

Maples was an old town, spread out across a wide shallow valley. It had a long-settled look; buildings had sagging roofs and plank walks that did not go from one building to the next. Most were clapboard with wooden awnings and few were two stories.

The first hotel they came to was the Jordan. It had been whitewashed probably only months before and someone had painted the wooden shutters blue. They were prominent along an alley that ran back from the street.

But a jarring note was the poster plastered to the wall beside the door, describing Reb, giving his name and particulars. He was worth four hundred dollars in Eversville.

Nothing was mentioned about dead or alive.

Tate looked at the poster and grinned. "What's your name here, Reb?"

"I guess it'd better be John Smith."

"John Smith, huh? Then you likely got a lot of owlhoot friends."

Reb laughed. "Henry Smith then, for the hotel register. What names d'you suppose the Collins boys will be using?"

"Maybe they ain't in a hotel."

That certainly was a possibility, Reb thought. They might have friends in town to stay with—it could be the reason they came here. And if so, it was going to be difficult to dig them out. Difficult to impossible.

They quickly determined the Collins boys were not in the hotels; bartenders had not seen them, or said they had not.

It was not unlikely they had gone through the town without stopping.

But the next morning Tate came down and sat by Reb in the restaurant.

"Collins is in town, Reb."

"How d'you know?"

Tate grinned. "Because last night I went upstairs with Rose, one of the girls. She told me the Collins boys held a party in the rooms over the saloon two days ago and she's seen them since."

"She volunteered this information?"

"Well, I ast her about them."

"Does she know where they're living?"

"I guess not."

Reb frowned, staring into the street. "You keep on seeing this girl—what's her name, Rose? See her every night and act like you're falling for her. Learn all you can. All right?"

Tate looked unhappy. "I ain't got the money to do that. She costs a dollar every time."

Reb pushed money across the table and Tate brightened. "Ever' night, Reb?"

"Yes, but don't be too obvious."

Tate nodded.

Rose had a broad, round face framed by curly blond hair. She was small, gave her age as twenty-four, if asked, and usually wore shiny black dresses that were cut low in front, a feature that love-starved pilgrims found fascinating, particularly because her frontal assets jiggled and wobbled delightfully when she moved, being restrained only by very sketchy coverings.

Of course such pilgrims were men just off the trail, usually smelling like mules or worse, wearing duds that were coated with dust, mud, and grease. They usually also wore beards and mustaches equally dusty and greasy. It took a girl with a strong stomach to get into bed with one.

Tate shaved and had a bath when he met Rose, and he had

money, so Rose encouraged his visits. Somewhere he had learned better manners, too. He did not wear his boots to bed.

When he asked her about Hop Collins, she quickly scented return business and replied that she had seen the man. She had no idea where he might be found. However, she agreed to try to worm that information from Collins. And thus kept Tate coming back.

But after the third day Reb began to be suspicious. The five saloon girls, including Rose, lived in a shanty behind the saloon and he had no trouble keeping it under his eye without being noticed. When they got up, around noon, they did simple chores, laundry mostly, and hung it out to dry. In the early evening they drifted into the saloon, ready for work. Reb saw everyone Rose talked to, a dozen or more men. She went upstairs with three or four, including Tate. There was only one way up and down.

When Tate came downstairs, he and Reb went out to the street at once. Tate said, "She seen him again today, Reb."

"She told you that?"

"She said she seen Hop. He come into the saloon, but left quick. She even had a word with him."

Reb shook his head. "She did not see him. That girl is milking us for whatever she can get."

Tate looked distressed. "Sure enough?"

"I doubt if she even knows the Collins boys. I watched her every minute."

Tate shook his head in disgust. "Shit. She made a fool outa me."

"Me too." Reb consoled him. "Me too."

It was a hard lesson. Whore girls could not be trusted. Reb blamed himself for being so gullible. He had wanted to believe her, that was the trouble. And now by this time the Collins brothers were long gone, the trail cold. There was nothing to do but go back to Cooper—and hopefully, be a little wiser next time.

* * *

But Shotgun declined to return. He was bound to go on south, he said, down into Texas to see kinfolk, since he was so close.

Reb and Tate took the trail north.

Because they were apparently the only beings on the road—they met no one at all—and since they were no longer chasing bandits, they did not bother to keep a watch when they slept at night.

The second night they both woke to a gruff command: "Roll out!"

Reb woke to find a six-shooter in his face. The man who held it was dressed in black. He smiled wickedly as Reb sat up and took Reb's .44. "Git your boots on."

"What is this?"

A second man got Tate out of the blankets. They had one of Reb's fliers, but had nothing on Tate. "This 'un can go."

They allowed no conversation between the two men, put Tate on his horse, and gave him his unloaded gun back. "Git a-goin'."

They were bounty hunters and had followed Reb and Tate from the town, waiting for a likely chance.

"We takin' you back to Eversville, partner. You can go peaceable or you can go hurt."

"I'm not worth anything to you dead."

"Who said anything about dead? Git on your horse."

The man in black was called Frenchy; the other was Sam. They never mentioned other names. Frenchy was obviously in charge, a lanky, gruff-talking man. Sam was short and dumpy, wearing a battered derby and ragged clothes. He was also a whiner, complaining constantly, utterances that Frenchy seldom replied to or acknowledged except with an occasional "shut up."

They headed eastward across the prairie. Frenchy did not bother to tie Reb's hands, which meant he had confidence in himself to prevent an escape attempt—with the cocked rifle resting across his thighs.

Reb was disgusted by the turn of events. Lady Luck had really given him the cold shoulder. Going back to prison was the last thing he wanted, and if he got there, it might well be his last act on earth. If Bad Ass was still a guard, his chances of living a week were slim. Bad Ass would shoot him for practice. Most likely with his glasses on.

Frenchy was taking him back for the four hundred dollars offered. He would probably reconsider if Reb offered five hundred; but Reb did not have five hundred. His only chance to avoid the leg irons was to escape. Somehow.

And the best possibility was Sam.

Sam was the weak link—but Frenchy knew it, too. Reb noticed that Frenchy watched Sam's every move.

Of course Frenchy knew nothing about him, Reb knew, but what he'd read on the posters. So he pretended to be nothing more than a bumbler. He did his best to look as if he were completely defeated and had given up, ready to go back. That act might bring him a chance. All he wanted was a slim chance. . . .

By the second day he thought Frenchy was accepting the act, letting down his guard just a bit.

The third morning, after breakfast, they came to a dry wash. Frenchy happened to be in the lead and went down the steep bank in a diagonal course. He went down fast, his horse surefooted, and turned to watch the others.

Reb was next and followed Frenchy's lead, reining in on the sand as Sam came over the edge. Sam did not follow them but came over, heading straight down. The horse slipped, tumbled, and pitched Sam out of the saddle. Sam yelped in surprise and terror as his mount went ass over teakettle.

Both hit the sand hard, and as Sam landed in a sprawl Reb was off his horse in a flying leap. He flung himself at Sam, grabbing Sam's revolver, all in the same fluid movement. He rolled, turning and firing at Frenchy—who fired back. But Frenchy was on a startled horse, Reb on his back on the solid ground. He put two bullets into Frenchy's heart, knocking the other from the saddle.

Then he turned to point the pistol at Sam. Sam shouted, "Don't shoot!" His hands shot up and his face paled. "This was Frenchy's idea, not mine!"

Reb got to his feet and motioned Sam up. He unloaded Sam's rifle and slammed it back into the boot. He looked down at Frenchy. Very dead.

"Put 'im on his horse."

Sam did as he was told, draping the lanky body over the saddle. Reb found his .44 in Frenchy's saddlebags, then unloaded Frenchy's rifle and slid it into the boot. He put Frenchy's Colt in his belt and told Sam to get moving.

"Where to?"

"Anywhere you want." Reb climbed on his horse and headed north. Half a mile away he looked back. Sam was still sitting the horse, staring after him.

16

He arrived back in Cooper only two days after Tate, who was astonished to see him. "What happened to them two bounty hunters?"

Reb told him. Jeff Larkin was delighted to see him as well though he was sorry they had lost the trail of the bank robbers. It was not possible to win every time, he said philosophically. He was also sorry that a man had lost his life for four hundred dollars. "It reminds me of the damn Welke brothers."

Larkin had served out his term of office that year and was retiring. He had already sold almost everything he owned and went around shaking hands and saying good-bye. He was heading back to St. Louis, and from there to the small town in Illinois where he had come from in the first place.

"I'm going to sit on the front porch in a rocker and watch folks go by," he said.

Reb went with him to the stage depot and saw him off.

With Larkin gone, he felt as if another page in his life had been turned. There was nothing else for him in Cooper. Reb said his own good-byes and rode north, heading for Rustin.

It had been months since he'd heard from his father.

The town did not look the same to him. He had the feeling it was slowly dying. There were fewer people on the streets and no soldiers at all. The army post had been closed.

Henry Jorganson had departed for Alabama with his wife.

Albe Newlan's store was open and Albe looked about the same, a little grayer, perhaps, and overjoyed to see him.

"Reb! You're a sight for sore eyes! Where'd you drop from?"

"Just thought I'd come home and say hello."

"You look bigger'n you was last time. You seen your pa yet?"

"I'm on my way there now. Is he all right?"

"He's fine. Was the last time I seen him two days ago."

"I see the fort has gone."

"Oh, they closed that up a year ago come March. Tryin' to sell the property, but nobody wants it. How long you goin' to stick around, Reb?"

"No idea." Reb smiled. "Till I get itchy to move on, I guess."

"They got a train goes all the way across the country now. You could go look at the Pacific Ocean." Albe sighed. "I never seen a ocean in my life."

Reb laughed. "I never thought of doing that."

"I thought of it a million times—sellin' this store and getting on a train."

Reb laid money on the counter. "Give me a bottle of good brandy to take home."

His father was astonished to see him. "For God's sake— Reb!" He pulled his son into the house, embracing him. "I was just thinking about you! Wondering where you were."

"I'm right here."

"Yes, you are, aren't you. Have you eaten? What've you got there, a bottle of whiskey?"

"Brandy. I stopped off to say hello to Albe." He put the bottle on a sideboard. "I see there's no more problems with soldiers."

"No, not for a long while. My, it's good to see you, Reb. You certainly look fit!"

"I am. Fine."

Todd chuckled. "And you've still got that old forty-four that Isham gave you. Are you hungry?"

"No." Reb looked around. "What've you done with the house?" The parlor was bare. Everything he remembered was gone, pictures off the walls and furniture.

"I didn't want to look at it," Todd said. "It was bad enough when your mother died. But after Isham—" He sighed deeply. "I just made some changes—put the things up in the attic." He took Reb's arm. "Come on in the kitchen. We'll open that bottle."

Reb discovered the next day that his father was seeing a widow in the town. She was a woman he had met in the local church; her husband was gone.

"Well, it gets lonely," Todd said. "A man needs someone to talk to."

Reb agreed, and tried to stay out of the way. He spent evenings in the Silver Dollar Saloon, and it took only a week of doing nothing for him to become almost too restless to sleep at night.

It was time to move on.

Todd deplored the idea, but realized there was very little in the long-settled town to interest a man who had seen the elephant. "Where you got it in mind to go from here?" his father asked one day.

"I don't know," Reb said honestly. "Albe suggested I go look at the Pacific Ocean."

"The ocean? What for?"

"Just to see it, I suppose."

"Hmm. Well, I saw Lake Erie once. I expect the ocean is pretty much like that, one hell of a lot of water."

Reb laughed. "I've seen pictures of it. I don't think I'll make the trip just to see."

He packed some food and set out in the morning. His father accompanied him to the edge of town and they said their good-byes. Reb promised to write.

This was a lot different from the time when he'd been hustled off to live with George and Oralia. That seemed a hundred years in the past. He was getting old. He was twenty-three.

He thought he would point toward Kansas City on the Missouri River. It was a big frontier town and ought to offer him employment. He still had a few dollars in his kick, enough to last a short while.

He met Shag Peters in the little town of Defiance. Reb stopped for the night and sat in on a quiet game of poker with Shag and two others. Shag was young, maybe twenty, lean and sandy-haired and amiable.

When the game broke up, they sat to drink a few beers before hitting the hay. Shag was thinking of going east to Kansas City, too, he said. He'd been working as a cowhand and had always wanted to see a town that had more than a thousand folks in it, one big enough to have horse cars and real music halls—with girls in tights. He'd seen pictures of such things in *Harper's Magazine*.

When Shag suggested they travel together, Reb agreed at once, glad of the company.

When they left the town behind next morning early, there was no road leading east; it was necessary to navigate partly by the sun and mostly by picking out a feature of the ground far ahead on the vast prairie and moving toward it—then doing the same thing again.

It was a land broken and rolling, seemingly limitless. Each night they drew a line in the dirt so they would know in the morning before the sun was up which direction they were headed.

The third day in late afternoon they began to look for a place to camp, one that had wood for a fire and grass for the horses. When they found a spot by a deep coulee, Shag slid off his horse—frowned and put his ear to the ground. He motioned to Reb. "Company . . ."

Reb nodded quickly—company could mean anything. He yanked the Winchester from the scabbard and pointed to the coulee. Shag led the horses into it as Reb lay down in the tall weeds, levering a shell into the chamber as quietly as he could.

They were on a slight rise with the ground sloping away toward the west with tall brush and weeds everywhere. He could feel the slight vibrations—hoofbeats—and in another moment the hairs on the back of his neck stood up.

A half-dozen painted Indians came out of the brush and moved toward him. They were several hundred yards away and he heard Shag's low whistle from behind. The band trotted their horses, chattering among themselves, led by a big, powerfully built man carrying a coup stick. There were no women or children among them; it was a war party, looking for trouble. Would they pass by?

They did not. Their leader halted suddenly and they all stopped, looking down. They had seen the fresh tracks of two horses!

They started toward him and Reb pressed himself into the ground, lying motionless, hearing the distant, guttural voices as they discussed the situation, looking about in all directions. Several got down to investigate the tracks more closely. They nodded and gestured, talking it over. Indians were great talkers, Reb knew. He hoped they would decide not to follow them.

A vain hope. Undoubtedly they would see that the tracks were of shod horses, which meant they had been made by horses belonging to white men. So their chances of catching two whites alone on the plains were excellent. They pointed in his direction and he gripped the Winchester tightly as they came toward him at a walk, the two in the lead leaning down to follow the tracks.

When they were within easy pistol shot, Reb got to his feet.

The Indians stopped instantly and were silent for a moment as they stared at him. Then they began to chatter again, looking behind him. They had seen the tracks of two horses. Where were they?

Reb held the Winchester prominently. They knew a repeating rifle when they saw one. He saw that most of them carried single-shooters, Sharps and old Springfields, even some caplocks. And they could see the six-shooter on his hip. He had twenty-one shots to their six.

The leader stared stonily at Reb. He wore a single eagle

feather in his black hair. His eyes were never still, moving here and there.

Then Shag spoke in a conversational tone. Instantly the Indians were silent, staring at the place the voice came from. He said, "Move back here, Reb. Walk slow."

Reb took a backward step, and as he did so several of the young bucks urged their ponies forward, possibly thinking to encircle him. Reb pointed the Winchester at them and they halted, growling to each other. They stared at him, black eyes in dark faces, hostile and eager.

Shag said again, "Come on—walk easy—don't let 'em make up their minds."

Reb took several steps and one of the braves let off a scream and whirled his rifle over his head. The others milled, raising dust.

"Let 'em yell," Shag said.

Another brave yelled and ran at him. Reb shouldered the rifle and the man danced the pony in a tight circle as the others surged forward a dozen steps. They were probably working themselves up to charge, he thought. But they probably didn't like the sight of the repeating rifle, and the other man might have one, too.

Reb moved backward. Another man ran at him and Reb almost fired. The brave turned aside, screaming, shaking his rifle.

They began to spread out, all yammering at once now, and one fired, the bullet whining over his head. They were apparently satisfied that they faced only two men. Would they charge in the face of the repeaters? Probably. They would duck down, making small targets on the ponies.

Shag said, "Only about ten feet, Reb . . . come on."

Reb glanced behind him. Shag was lying on an upslope, the rifle at his shoulder. His cocked pistol was lying in front of him.

As Reb turned his head they came—howling and shrilling like demons.

Shag fired and the leading brave toppled. Reb fired as fast as he could work the lever. Two horses were down, kicking and screaming. Dust boiled and the air was full of lead. All of them had fired at once—and now they scattered, leaving three down on the field.

One horse was dead, the other still kicking and making a terrible sound. Reb went to it and fired and the kicking stopped.

Shag jumped up and began to reload. "Damn me, they shouldn't have tried that." He nudged the fallen braves with his toe. "They dead."

The others had disappeared in the brush. "They'll be back for the bodies," Reb said. "Let's make tracks."

They jogged into the coulee, mounted, and headed east. They had been lucky, neither of them hit. But Indians were not known to be sharpshooters. Probably the old punkin-slingers they had wouldn't shoot straight anyway. And they probably never practiced.

17

Henton was a dusty little town on the high plains, POP: 542, a sign told them. But it had a hotel of sorts and a small bath house with a copper tub, where Reb scrubbed himself with a bar of hard yellow soap.

The hotel had a tiny restaurant on one side, a counter and two tables, run by the wife of the hotel owner, and a deadfall on the other. Reb and Shag had steaks and coffee and went into the saloon for beer.

It was a modest place, the only saloon in town; it had a long bar and tables where a few men were playing cards and chatting. There were two doors at the back, one stood wide open, the way to the privies behind the building. The other was ajar, showing steps up to the second floor. Probably, Reb thought, there were girls upstairs, making a hard living on the bunks.

A painted girl was playing the off-key piano, surrounded by several young men trying to sing. And in the middle of the song a woman came into the room from the stairs.

This one, Reb saw at once, was no ordinary saloon girl. She was tall and dark and tastefully dressed in a long, dark blue gown with a necklace of small bright stones. She went behind the bar to talk with the bartender, both poring over papers; the woman made notes, then went to a table in the rear and an aproned boy served her a supper that probably came from the restaurant. It was on a covered tray that he brought from the outside door.

Shag noticed her, too. "Probably the owner's wife, huh?"

111

"Yes, most likely." A damn good-looking woman. A rarity on the plains, especially in such a little burg as Henton. She might well be the only woman in town, not counting saloon whores.

Her name, he learned before they went back to the hotel, was Hetty, and she owned the saloon.

Hester Griffen and her husband had come to Henton five years before, Reb was told, and had bought the saloon. The husband believed the town would prosper and grow—it had not.

Unfortunately he had died, hit by a stray bullet from a saloon fight. He'd been tending bar at the time. A drunk had pulled a gun and fired in the general direction of a gambler, who had centered him with a derringer. Hetty's husband had been buried in the local boot hill, along with the drunk.

She had been forced either to sell out or run the saloon. There had been no takers, so she ran it and succeeded. Men rode miles and miles just to look at her, and maybe to exchange a word or two.

In the two years since her husband's death, she had received hundreds of marriage proposals. She was the most beautiful woman in the territory—no one denied it—in a land where beautiful women were almost nonexistent.

And she had a bit of money put aside.

But none of the suitors suited her. She took none of them seriously.

A troop of cavalry, some thirty men, came through the town the next day. The hostiles were out, the lieutenant said. He strongly advised against people traveling alone or in small numbers on the plains. He was heading west and offered to escort anyone bound in that direction.

"We was lucky," Tate said, watching the soldiers dismount in the street. "We only met a half dozen of 'em. A real war party would've had our hair."

Reb agreed. If those half dozen had not been so impetuous, and had concentrated on finding their horses, putting them afoot, it might easily have turned out differently.

But wagon trains were still moving. Reb found one making up in the main street; he talked to the wagon master, who readily agreed to take them along. He was glad of two more Winchesters. They would leave, he said, the next morning at sunup.

Hetty also made arrangements with the wagon master to take her to Mellis, the next town, a two-day journey. She went there as a rule every two weeks, ostensibly to go shopping. There were shops and stores in Mellis that did not exist in Henton.

But her main reason was the bank. There was none in Henton either. She carried saloon receipts in a homemade money belt worn about her waist under her dress and coat.

Inside the coat was also a home-sewn leather sheath into which she slipped a double-action revolver—which she knew how to use. A young bodyguard usually accompanied her and she nearly always went with a wagon train. But today the young man was sick in bed.

The eleven-wagon train was parked on the road out of town, its stock in nearby corrals. As she walked to it in the chilly dawn she watched the hostlers hooking up. She would ride in a trap wagon, the smallest in the train. The driver, a youngster of perhaps fifteen, helped her up over the wheel and handed up her bag as she settled herself in a duster. She tied a flowered square of cloth over her dark hair; it would be dusty, of course, and she would have to wash it in rain-water when she got back.

When all was ready, the driver climbed up beside her. He was a shy boy named José, not a conversationalist. Hetty resigned herself to another long, tedious trip.

Three hours out from Henton they crossed a wide area where the grass and brush had been burned off; the smell of it was very strong. To the south were patches of wildflowers, yellow and red blushes in the brown buffalo grass. Beyond were smudged traces on the horizon, blue and hazy hills.

At the midday stop Hetty climbed down over the wheel, and as she brushed dust from her skirts a tall, lean man offered her a tin cup of coffee. She turned to smile, accepting it, "Thank you, Mister . . . ?"

"They call me Reb, Miss Hetty."

"Reb? Short for Rebel?"

"I reckon so."

"You're too young to have been a rebel in the war."

He laughed. "Thank goodness I was. That was some war! I think it was my uncle Isham who fastened that name onto me—when I was too young to object."

"I see."

Several of the wagon men built small fires and broiled strips of meat. One of them gave her a plate with meat and crackers on it. She leaned against a wagon on the shady side and ate slowly, watching Reb. He was definitely different from the rest of the men, a subtle difference but apparent. He was not one of the wagon-train handlers, but was traveling with them, as she was.

He looked to be about twenty-three, two years younger than she. He had straight brown hair and gray eyes and a long scar on his left cheek. She wondered about the scar. He had a well-worn pistol on his hip—was he a gunman? No, not likely. She had seen many of that stripe in the saloon and Reb did not fit the image, though he looked very capable. She saw how the other men respected him.

When the wagons moved out, she asked José beside her if he knew Reb.

The boy shook his head. "But I heard 'em talking. He been a deputy over to Cooper."

"A deputy sheriff?"

"Yes, ma'am." He glanced at her. "And he been in prison. Least, that's what they say."

"How could he be a deputy and also be in prison? Are you saying he was a prisoner?"

José shrugged. "Maybe he was a prison guard, I dunno. But they say he damn good with that pistol." He coughed. "Oh, pardon me, Miss Hetty."

She tied the scarf more tightly about her head. Prison? There must be some mistake about that. He was like no prisoner she had ever seen.

There were eyes everywhere, including mounted men far out to the sides, looking for movement. Human eyes catch movement very quickly, no matter how small. But they saw nothing curious or hostile that afternoon.

"It's sure empty country," one said when the scouts returned.

In due course the sun dropped far down in the west and the wagons circled for safety with the stock inside. A few men took grain sacks and went out to mine surface coal— buffalo chips—for the evening cookfires.

The men said that camp cooking was not for ladies, so Hetty stayed out of the way. She was not particularly hungry anyway. But then Reb paused by the trap wagon and smiled at her. "Want something to eat?"

She smiled back. "I'm starving," she said.

Mellis had the look of a young town. It was better kept up than many, Reb thought. Of course there were old buildings, but most were not falling down or badly weathered. Civic pride was a new idea, but it must have taken root here.

Tate, who declared himself flat broke, found a job almost immediately, deciding to work awhile to build up his cash reserves. Reb signed for a room in a small hotel and discovered that Hetty was a neighbor, just down the hall.

They walked to the restaurant and had supper together and she told him she had been staying in that hotel when she came to town for nearly two years.

She dressed very simply; she had brought but one smallish bag with her from Henton. It probably contained, he thought, only one change of clothes. He asked if she was shopping for clothes in Mellis and she said she bought only material and did her own dressmaking. "I do the sewing in my spare time at home. You men have your hobbies. I have my sewing basket."

He said, "I'm surprised you've stayed so long in Henton."

"The saloon is a living."

"You could sell it and go east."

She made a futile little gesture. "Not many are interested in buying. My husband thought the town would grow. There was talk of a stage line that never came true. I'm getting by now, but I would sell if a reasonable offer came my way."

"Do you have family in the East?"

"Yes, my parents are still living—in Pennsylvania. My mother and I write every month. I would go there if I left Henton. There's no other family. I never knew my husband's. What about you?"

"My father is all that's left of my family."

"They tell me you were a deputy sheriff."

He looked at her curiously. Had she asked about him? "Yes, I've been a deputy in several towns."

"They also said you were in prison."

Reb smiled. "You've been listening to gossip. But yes, it's true, I was. However, I was innocent of the charge, and when I got the chance, I broke out."

Her eyes widened. "You're a wanted man?"

"Yes, in certain areas. Not here. At least I haven't seen any posters with my name on them."

"I hope you don't. . . ."

They lingered over supper, then Hetty returned to her room and he looked into the stable to see that his horse was cared for. The stableboy had gone, and the horse was fine.

He went upstairs and along the hall to his room.

Hetty stood in the open door of her room and he paused, gazing at her. She said, "I was waiting for you. . . ."

He went inside and she closed and bolted the door.

Gunther Frick, a big, imposing man, was a rancher, used to taking what he wanted. He had, over the years, driven off any number of squatters who had settled on his range . . . what he considered to be his range, though he did not own it.

The squatters had wisely chosen to move rather than face the various inconveniences that Gunny—as he was always called—was capable of furnishing, such as ruined crops and burned barns. Gunny hated plows. As he and many ranchers were fond of saying: "The prairie sod was right side up in the first place."

Gunny got most of what he went after. He was tenacious and persistent . . . with a mean streak. His wife had died after battling him for thirty years—and finally lost. She had not given him either a son or daughter and of course he blamed her for it.

But one desire he went after, he did not get. And was not likely to get. Hetty Griffen. She wanted no part of him, and had told him so possibly a hundred times. But her denials were as the falling rain to a pond. Gunny had made up his mind; he wanted her. She would have to agree—sooner or later.

And as luck would have it, he was in Mellis when she came in with the wagon train. He was closeted with a banker, talking loans, and did not know it till the next day.

Then one of the cowhands he had brought with him told him that Miss Hetty had spent the night in the hotel with a man.

Gunny was enraged.

Who was the man?

His name, they told him, was Rebel. He was a drifter.

Gunny stormed into the hotel. But the man, Rebel, was not there. He had not checked out, the clerk said, but he was gone . . . somewhere.

Gunny took the stairs two at a time and pounded on Hetty's door. When she opened it, he strode in and slammed it behind him. "You whore!" he yelled. "Sleeping with a goddamn drifter!"

Hetty was astonished. She pointed to the door. "Get out of here, Gunny Frick!"

He backhanded her, knocking her against the wall, and she slid down in a heap, seeing stars. Grabbing her arm, he yanked her up and hit her again. She fell unconscious across the bed. He shouted at her and punched her, pulling her off the floor. He slapped her face hard and, when she did not answer or open her eyes, cursed and went out, slamming the door.

He had brought three cowhands with him into town. He ordered them to find the man Rebel. Then he sat in the saloon with a revolver on the table before him.

18

The wagon train was still in Mellis; two wagons had troubles, one with an axle, another with a wheel. The iron rim had loosened and had to be sweated on again by the blacksmith.

Paco, one of Gunny's hands, asked the wagon master about Rebel.

"A dangerous man," the wagon master replied. "He's the one gunned down Peter Hinch—in a fair fight. I thought ever'body knew that."

"Hinch! Jesus! I never knew it. That's for sure?"

"Damn sure."

Paco told his two companions, "This hombre Rebel is a gunslick. Gunny ain't payin' me to get dead. I don't think he's in town—do you?"

They all quickly agreed the man Rebel could not be located.

Paco told Gunny, who growled at him.

Reb entered the hotel and went immediately to his room to wash up. Then he walked down the hall to Hetty's room and rapped on the door. No answer.

She was probably out, looking in the stores. He could not have said why he turned the knob. He was mildly surprised to find the door open. He looked inside, seeing no one.

But a chair was lying on its side.

He closed the door behind him and walked into the room.

Hetty was on the floor behind the bed! With an exclamation, he knelt by her—she was badly beaten!

But she was alive—with a huge bruise alongside her head and others on her face and arms. He poured cold water into the basin and bathed her face, then gently lifted her onto the bed.

In a little while she opened her eyes wearily.

He said, "Who did this to you?"

She struggled to answer. It took several minutes before she could get the word out. "Gunny . . ."

"Gunny?" Who the hell was that?

She nodded and closed her eyes.

He unfastened and removed most of her clothes and slid her into the bed. She was breathing shallowly.

He ran downstairs and asked the clerk if the town had a doctor.

"There's one, but he ain't worth a damn. Nobody goes to see him because he's always drunk. Folks goes to the doc over to Bickers. They run this one out of Ohio."

"Do you know somebody named Gunny?"

"Sure. That's Gunny Frick."

"Where can I find him?"

The clerk made a face. "Maybe in the saloon."

The clerk was right about the doctor. Reb found him, drunk and useless.

He went into the saloon and stood by the door, frowning at the room. "I'm looking for Gunny."

He said it good and loud and everyone turned. A bartender said, "He left awhile ago."

"You know where he went?"

The man shrugged. "Maybe home. But I dunno where that is."

No one else knew either.

He returned to the hotel. He had kept the door key and entered the room to find Hetty apparently asleep, moaning softly. She was obviously in pain and there was nothing he could do for her.

He sat by her that night. In the morning she was worse, the bruises enlarged and blacker. Gunny had hit her very hard, the son of a bitch. Reb wondered why. He brought her soup and fed it to her, though she wanted little. He bathed her face and the bruises and she told him in halting phrases about Gunny Frick.

Gunny owned a ranch outside of Henton, she said, and had been pushing his intentions on her since her husband died. He apparently considered her his property, no matter her feelings about it.

She finally drifted off to a restless sleep that afternoon. Late in the evening he tried to wake her to sip a bit more soup. But she did not wake easily and he did not want to shake her. . . .

He sat in a chair beside her bed that night, dozing and sleeping.

In the morning when he woke, she was pale and cold. She had slipped away in the night; she was dead.

Hetty's body was buried in Mellis on a chill, overcast day. Immediately afterward, without waiting for companions or escort, Reb left for Henton, riding alone, with a rage boiling inside him. Gunny Frick would pay for the death of a beautiful woman who had harmed no one.

He crossed the prairie, careless of tracks, and arrived in Henton in the middle of the afternoon to ask questions. A blacksmith took him into the street and pointed south.

"Gunny lives about ten miles thataway. Near six mile you'll come to Frypan Crick. Jus' foller it to the house."

"Thanks."

He rode south at once. The creek was a shallow stream, maybe fifteen feet at the widest; the horse splashed across and he saw the house at dusk. It was a long, low adobe-and-log building with two chimneys. He could see a light glimmering inside; someone was home. Off to the right was a barn and corrals and a line of sheds. Behind the house he could make out part of the bunkhouse.

Reb slid the rifle into the scabbard and got down in front of the house door, rapping on it. The heavy door was opened by an older, white-haired man who looked at him with raised brows.

"I want to see Gunny," Reb said.

"He ain't here."

Reb pushed by him. "I'd like to make sure."

The man scowled. "You can't come in here like that!"

Reb ignored him and walked into a large parlor. The walls were decorated with hunting trophy heads. A fire was burning briskly in a huge fieldstone fireplace. A bottle waited on a sideboard with two glasses.

Was the man lying about Gunny not being home?

A stout woman came to a door on the far side of the room and stared at him.

Reb said to her, "Where's Gunny?"

The man snapped, "I told you—he's not here."

The woman asked, "Who are you?"

"They call me Reb." He went past the woman into a hallway and looked into the rooms off it. There were three bedrooms, all apparently empty. At the end of the hall was a kitchen, and a boy who stared at him with round eyes, then ran out the back and slammed the door.

Reb went back to the parlor and faced the man. "Where can I find Gunny?"

"What you want him for?"

"He killed a friend of mine. I want to discuss it with him."

"Gunny did?"

"Where is he?"

"I—I don't know."

The front door opened and two men entered and Reb turned to face them. They looked like ordinary cowhands; one carried a carbine, the other had a pistol in his belt.

The white-haired man said quickly, "He pushed in here, lookin' for Gunny."

The taller of the two men said gruffly, "You—git on outside."

Reb opened his coat, revealing the .44. He spoke softly. "Don't get yourselves dead over something that's not your affair."

There was a silence as both men eyed him, sizing him up. The tall one blinked and the other licked his lips.

Then without warning, a shot came from the doorway where the woman had stood. The bullet smashed a lamp beside Reb. He whirled and fired as a second shot slammed into the wall. Reb fired once more, seeing a large man stumble and go to his knees. Where had he come from— hiding in one of the bedrooms? He must be Gunny. The man knocked over a chair and sprawled on the puncheon floor.

The tall man ran to Gunny and knelt. In a moment he stood and shook his head. Reb could hear the woman moaning in the hall. He motioned the man with the carbine away from the door.

"An eye for an eye," Reb said, and went out to his horse. He rode away from the house.

Justice of a sort had been done—or rather, Hetty had been avenged. But it was not very satisfying. She deserved much better.

He went back to Mellis and sat in a saloon with a bottle in front of him, feeling very low. He was not a drinking man; had never been drunk in his life. He had seen plenty of drunks and even felt sorry for some of them, knowing why a few had come to that state. He never expected to follow them.

Hetty was dead. Beautiful Hetty was gone for good; she would never return. And the man who had knocked her around and ultimately killed her was gone, too. Good riddance. Her death affected him a great deal, much more than he would have suspected. And it had been so sudden.

She had been so alive. Her smile had delighted his soul . . . it had brightened the drab surroundings. He had known her for such a brief period, only a few days. It was odd how a moment in time could mean so much.

He blamed himself for not being with her when Gunny had shown up. It would never have happened. Of course he had not known Gunny existed—but he still blamed himself.

That was why he drank himself into a stupor—to drive away the terrible thoughts. He had to be carried up to his room and dumped on the bed.

He woke the next day with a miserable headache. He was fully dressed and had no idea how he had come to be on the bed when his last memory was the saloon.

He felt utterly desolate and nothing seemed to help. Was this what drunks went through constantly? He remained sprawled on the bed, unmoving, doing his best to keep all thoughts out of his head. Especially those of her.

But nothing helped.

The day wore on, and in the afternoon his head began to feel slightly better. How much had he drunk? He was hungry and thinking about crawling out of bed and splashing water onto his face.

Then the door opened and two men came in. They both wore stars on their shirts. One said, "You the kid they call Reb?"

"Yes . . ."

"Then you under arrest for the killin' of Gunny Frick."

They put him in the town jail and he lay on a cot, gritting his teeth against the throbbing pain in his head. It was worse now.

But the next day he began to feel better. His strong body fought the liquor and was winning. A deputy told him one of the riders from Gunny's ranch had accused him. The word had been telegraphed around and he had been found in Mellis. He would be sent back to Henton.

"They say you pushed your way into the house and shot Gunny."

"Gunny fired first," Reb said.

"That's for the judge to decide."

19

Reb made the trip in a barred wagon. He was alone behind the bars; two heavily armed horsemen accompanied the driver. They went with an escort of cavalrymen and arrived without incident.

Details of the case had preceded him and Reb quickly discovered that opinions in the town favored him over Gunny. Gunny's treatment of Hetty Griffen in other days was known. Everyone was willing to believe the worst about him in this.

Henton wasn't much of a town, but it had a good, stout jail. There were four cells, two on either side of an aisle.

The building was fieldstone, two feet thick, the roof was made of logs with dirt piled atop them. Reb looked it over and knew he would not break out with anything less than a twelve-pounder cannon.

The case had garnered some interest and the sheriff himself came from the county seat to look at him in the cell. "How many witnesses to the shooting?" he demanded.

"Three, not counting myself," Reb said.

The sheriff nodded. Apparently that agreed with what he had been told.

The town deputy was a kindly, middle-aged man named Luke Seider. "I knew Gunny," he said to Reb, when he brought the prisoner's supper. "I guess ever'body hereabouts knew him. He was a ring-tailed son of a bitch. I doubt if they're going to find a jury that'll convict anybody who done

126

what you did. I figger you could've buried him in a anthill and poured syrup over him and they'd set you free.''

"When will the judge get here?"

Luke shrugged. "Week or so, I reckon. Hard to guess. He ain't been here in Henton for more'n a year. We don't have the kind of crime that needs a judge. You play cribbage?"

"No, but you can teach me. It looks like we'll have time."

The judge arrived in ten days, riding a roan horse and accompanied by three wagons hauling freight farther south. He put up at the hotel and spent the first evening in the saloon, sitting alone, sipping whiskey and playing solitaire. He was a tall, bearded man dressed in black, with shiny black boots.

He set up his court the next day in the saloon, it being the largest room in the town. A jury of nine men was selected after the judge questioned nearly a hundred. He could not find twelve who were acceptable to both sides.

In the afternoon he heard a number of cases involving land purchases, sales, debts, and mortgages, and one case of claim jumping that turned out to be a misunderstanding.

Reb's case was called the following day and he was told to recite the facts as he knew them, which he did in an even tone: "I went to call on Gunther Frick because he had killed Hetty Griffen."

The judge asked, "How do you know he killed her?"

"Because she told me. He was the one who beat her so severely she died."

"And what did you intend, when you went to call on Mr. Frick?"

Reb hesitated. "I'm not sure. I knew I couldn't let him get away with it . . . but I didn't intend killing him out of hand. I had it in mind to bring him into town."

"But you didn't."

"No. When he fired at me, he settled the matter."

"Would you have beaten him?"

Reb took a long breath. "I have to tell you it crossed my

mind—and I'm not sure I wouldn't have. I was in rather a
state. Her death affected me a great deal.''

The three witnesses were called, one at a time. The white-
haired man was a cousin. He declared that Reb had come to
kill Gunny.

Reb said loudly, "How did you know what was in my
mind?''

The judge's gavel hit the table, but he frowned at the
cousin. "Please stick to the facts. Did Mr. Wiley say to you
that he intended to kill Mr. Frick?''

The cousin sighed. "No . . . no, he didn't.''

The two cowhands were called and each told the same
story. The boy had come running to the bunkhouse to tell
them someone had come gunning for their boss. They had
entered the house to find Reb there.

"Then what happened?''

"Gunny showed up all of a sudden and took a couple shots
at this'un. The defendant.''

The judge said, "Mr. Frick fired first?''

Both cowhands agreed. "Yes, he did.''

The judge insisted they tell every detail, that Gunny had
suddenly appeared and fired and Reb had then drawn his
pistol and fired back.

He then questioned the cousin again. "Is this true? Mr.
Frick fired first?''

The cousin admitted it was so.

The judge said, "Then I instruct the jury to find for the
defendant. This is clearly a case of self-defense.''

The jury complied without leaving the room.

Reb was free to go.

Reb sat in the Merchants' Saloon with a mug of coffee at
his elbow, shuffling a greasy pack of cards listlessly. He had
not been in love with Hetty—as far as he knew what love
was—had he? He had been terribly fond of her, but the idea
that he would never see her again was what mattered.

Her passing would mean an enormous difference. He
thought back over the things they'd said to each other, the

little things she'd done, the way she'd looked at him—all the million and one tiny bits—that were gone forever.

He laid the cards out to play solitaire—then swept them up again. He had no patience with cards. . . .

A man came through the swinging doors of the saloon and Reb watched him lean over the bar, talking to the bartender. The barman looked around the room, then pointed, and the man came across to stand in front of the table.

"You're Reb Wiley, sir?"

He was dressed in worn jeans, checked shirt under a leather coat, and looked to be unarmed.

Reb nodded. "What is it?"

"May I sit down?"

"By all means," Reb said. "Help yourself."

The stranger pulled out a chair and sat. "My name's Fred Davis, Mr. Wiley. I've got three wagons out in the street and we want to go to Santa Paula."

"Yes?"

Davis smiled. "I'd like to hire your gun to go along with us."

Reb looked at him curiously. A very ordinary-appearing man, clean-shaven with sparse hair, neatly dressed though his clothes were not new. He said, "What's in the wagons?"

Davis said, "A printing press and equipment mostly. I'm going to start a newspaper in Santa Paula."

"Three wagons . . . How many of you in all?"

"Eight."

"How many rifles?"

"All of us can shoot, Mr. Wiley, except my daughter. She's barely seven. We are three couples and a boy, fifteen."

He thought about it. Santa Paula was probably a hundred miles south and west as the crow flew. He fiddled with the cards, thinking about Kansas City; Santa Paula was in the opposite direction. However, he did need money, and this looked to be an easy job. They probably wanted him to act as scout, and maybe to bring in a bit of meat.

"We can pay fifty dollars," Davis said. "And food, of course."

"Why me?" Reb asked.

Davis smiled again. "They tell me you're the best man with a gun in all the territory."

He went out to look at the wagons. As he expected, they were farm wagons, strengthened with high axles and pulled by mules. The people were standing in a group, looking at him hopefully. Davis introduced them and he shook with the men; the boy stared at him as if he might be someone famous.

Mrs. Davis was a comely blond woman; another couple was named Parsons and the third, Kelloway. The boy was John Kelloway and Davis's daughter was Maud. They had all come from Kansas and were eager to complete the journey, as Davis said, to begin living in houses again.

Reb glanced at the sky. It was late afternoon. "When d'you want to start?"

They rolled out of town at sunup, with Reb leading, a Winchester across his thighs. Their enemy would be hostile Indians, he was certain. The three men were well armed, with pistols and rifles; indeed, they had already had a brush with Indians, Davis said, and had come off well. He thought they had been lucky.

Reb led them along a well-worn path for the first day, till it turned eastward. Then they struck out across the prairie, navigating by the stars and by landmarks.

Davis had been in communication with a number of merchants, he told Reb, and had agreed to start a newspaper in their town. One of the wagons contained the press and equipment, a stone, a few cases of type, and a cylinder. He had published a paper in Indiana, but had been driven out of business by a competitor who had been better financed. The merchants in Santa Paula were willing to furnish him with a building and houses.

Publishing a newspaper, especially on the frontier, Davis said, was not a way to get rich, but he expected to make beans for his family and his helpers. They would grow with the community.

They wound through low scrub-covered hills and came out on the high plains again, with empty horizons on every side. Reb roved ahead and came back within view of the plodding wagons now and again. His worry was that hostiles would rush them—but they did not.

When they stopped at night, he saw that they dug pits for the cooking fires so they could not be seen beyond the wagons. The second night they halted beside a sheet of brown water that was bordered by saw grass, cattails, and a few drowned cottonwoods.

The fires were put out as soon as the cooking was finished and Reb arranged the night watches. The third night, under an ice-white moon, was uneventful.

Trouble came the next day, just before noon.

Reb was far out to the side when he heard the first shot. Turning, he put spurs to his horse instantly and galloped back to the wagons, yanking out the Winchester.

Two more shots came before he had the wagons in view. Then, as he spurred the horse over a rise, three men galloped away from the wagons as if they had seen him, toward the north.

Reb reined in at the wagons and Davis appeared, looking very glum. "They robbed us—took everything we had."

"How did it happen?"

"We thought they were friends—they came in smiling, then the guns threatened us."

"What was the firing?"

"I think they meant to cow us. Nobody is hurt."

"All right." Reb nodded. "Stay here." He put spurs to the horse, following the trail of the robbers. When he reached the first rise, he saw them, probably two miles distant, still heading north.

He followed all afternoon, closing only slightly.

When the shadows began to lengthen, he slowed his pace, watching for an ambush. One well-placed bullet would put him afoot. He was sure they had seen him—unless they never looked behind. And if they had seen him, they would certainly try to stop him.

They had followed the same course since leaving the wagons—probably they had come on the three wagons by accident and decided to improve their purses—so they were possibly heading toward a particular place. Maybe a town.

Of course they might easily change the course as soon as it got dark—or they might think to outrun him. He had never seen them except at a great distance and could not recognize them. They would figure themselves safe in a town around other people.

He could not let them get to a town.

It was impossible to know if they stopped for the night or not. Reb rode a wide circle around where he thought they might be and continued on through the rest of the night, walking the horse. He hoped to be in front of them come daylight.

And he was.

They had halted. Reb saw them first a mile or so distant. He lay down on a rounded hill and waited for them to come close.

When they were within a hundred yards, he got to his feet, holding the Winchester. The three stopped instantly and Reb yelled, "I want what you took from the wagons."

At once, as though on command, they scattered. Reb sighted on the one in the center and fired, knocking him from the saddle. He fired at the rider on the right, aiming at the horse, causing it to stumble and fall. The man sprang free and fired a quick shot. Reb's shot spun him around and he dropped the rifle.

The third man galloped away. Reb jumped on his horse and followed, firing when he got close, working the lever, emptying the rifle magazine. The horse swerved into tall brush and fell heavily. The man lay squirming.

Sliding off the horse, Reb dragged the bandit by the boots out of the brush. He had been hit in the side. Reb put a revolver under his chin.

"Let's have what you took from the wagons."

The man stammered and indicated his coat pockets and Reb turned them out. Rings and two watches and a roll of money. He pocketed all of it. "Is that all?"

The man's eyes rounded and he stared into the muzzle of the pistol, obviously scared to death. "It's—it's all—"

Reb tossed the man's pistol into the brush and mounted the bay horse, galloping back to the others. One was dead, the other hit in the right shoulder. One horse was dead and the man glared at him. "Who're you anyways?"

Reb grinned at him. "Turn your pockets out."

The man hesitated and Reb drew and fired. The bullet whistled by the other's ear and he quickly pointed to the downed horse with a shaking finger. "Saddlebags . . ."

Reb pulled the saddlebags off and looked inside. Money and jewelry. He fastened the straps again.

The man said, "It ain't all theirs! Some of that's mine!"

"Izzat so?" Reb said. "When I count it up, I expect it'll just exactly cover my fee."

The man sat on the ground, all the fire out of him. "I'm hurt bad. You going to leave me here?"

Reb swung up on the bay and looked down at him. "You're lucky I don't bury you out here, you son of a bitch."

He spurred back toward the wagons.

20

Fred Davis and the others were overjoyed to see Reb return in one piece. "Did you meet up with them?"

"I met them," Reb replied. He unloaded the money and jewels onto a blanket spread on the grass, to delighted exclamations. But when they picked through it, Davis said, "There's more here than they took from us."

Reb smiled. "Yes, I know. They agreed that anything extra was my fee."

Davis stared at him. "They agreed?"

"Without reservation."

Fred said, "Is there something you aren't telling us, Reb?"

Reb laughed. "You don't want to hear all of it. Let's leave it as is."

He pocketed more than a hundred dollars.

They reached Santa Paula three days later without further incident. The building that Davis and his people had been promised was not new but very serviceable. It was the size of a small barn and had been used as a boot-and-leather shop and a residence. The large sign in the shape of a boot was still out front.

Santa Paula seemed a pleasant little town and Reb stayed for several days. When he began to think about returning, a troop of cavalry rode in. They put up tents in the center of the town, in a square, and Reb talked to the lieutenant.

The troop was bound for Fort Dodge in Kansas. A wagon train was forming in a meadow outside the town and the lieutenant agreed to escort them eastward. Reb was invited to join along with a few other riders.

The lieutenant, some years out of West Point, was a lean, whipcord-wiry young man who obviously knew his business. He had thirty-five men, including two drivers and two light wagons hauling their baggage, tents, bedrolls, personal effects, ration and ammunition boxes.

The column had one scout, a stocky Mexican named Tomas Rivera, who wore a long-fringed buckskin jacket and fringed buckskin trousers shoved into loose soft leggins over cowhide boots with high heels.

Reb talked to him at length. They had seen no hostiles, Tomas said, though he had cut sign several times. "They watchin' us," he said. "But the lootenant don't let nobody straggle."

With the bluecoats guarding them it was an uneventful journey to Ayres, a railroad town. The wagons needed various repairs and laid over half a day while the farrier's hammers banged against anvils under workshops.

Reb walked through the depot and came face-to-face with a line of wanted posters. One jumped out at him: WANTED FOR MURDER $1000 REWARD! *Hop Collins. Alias Hank Connors, alias Heck Cluny. Armed and dangerous.*

There followed a short description: Collins was black-haired and stocky with an eagle tattoo on the back of his right hand. The reward would be paid for information leading to his arrest and conviction.

Hop Collins! The same man who had shot to death Martin Finerty, the bank president. The same man who, with his brother, Ames, had given him and the posse the slip.

The poster also noted that Collins had shot two people on the local stage during a robbery. He was wanted dead or alive.

Reb rubbed his jaw. One thousand dollars reward . . . Not a bad grubstake. He looked up the local law, a man named Bert Newcome, who was of the opinion that Collins was in the vicinity.

"He got cousins living not far out of town," he told Reb,

"and I think he stays here now and then. The only trouble is, they's a dozen ways in and out. It'd take a damn regiment to surround the place."

Reb asked directions and rode to look over the cousin's farm. It was a ramshackle place with a half-dozen houses and sheds and a barn; much of the ground was unused and overgrown with weeds as if no one ever cared for it. The houses were mostly hidden by trees and brush; no one seemed to be home.

He wormed his way close enough to see corrals and chicken coops and finally a few men who moved from one shed to another, but none of them was Collins.

Maybe Collins wasn't here at the moment.

He gave up the watch when the light began to fade. He thought of moving in closer, but the sight of a few dogs near the houses decided him otherwise.

Reb went back the next day and kept up his surveillance of the cousin's farm, spending hours on his belly in the brush with field glasses, trying to determine if Hop was there or not. If he were in one of the houses, he certainly stayed inside—at least during the day.

And then to his disgust, he learned from Deputy Newcome that Collins had gotten into a fight in Hanford, a nearby town, and shot up a saloon with his brother, Ames. Newcome said there was no doubt it had been Collins. Half a dozen had seen him.

Reb hurried there immediately, arriving a day late. Collins was no longer in town; the outlaws had been seen hightailing it toward the east . . . and there were any number of towns in that direction.

Reb hurried to the closest, but the Collins boys had not been there. They had held up a store in Lennon, twenty miles to the north, and shot a bystander.

When he got there, the bystander had died. The storekeeper told him the two owlhoots had come in to buy vittles.

"They was just as nice as you please," the merchant said. "Then Joe—he was standin' over by the door—he says, 'Them two're the Collins boys!' " The storekeeper pantomimed drawing a pistol. "One of 'em turned and shot Joe three times, *bam, bam, bam*, just like that, without sayin' a word. I thought they was goin' to shoot me, too, but they just took m'money box and skedaddled."

Reb said, "There's no doubt who they were?"

"Hell no. It was the Collins brothers, all right. I seen pitchers of Hop."

"Stocky and black-headed . . ."

"Yeah, that's him. With that tattoo. His brother is a inch or two taller and got brown hair. And they both mean as snakes."

"How much money did they get from you?"

"Not much, only a few dollars. I don't keep much in the box. A lot of folks pays by the month, you know."

From the store, the two brothers had gone into a deadfall in Lennon, bold as brass, and spent the afternoon drinking, defying the law to come in after them. The town marshal was a man twice their age and not a gunman. He had not been hired to face gunslicks and he declined to become a target.

Reb talked to the owner of the deadfall, who said, "They sat there playin' cards and drinking the whole damn afternoon, with guns on the table. Now'n then one of them would shoot a few holes in the ceilin'." He pointed. "They got a big kick outta shootin' holes in her."

Reb looked up. There was a large, rather crude painting of a very naked girl on the ceiling. Her pubic area had been shot to shreds.

The owner said, "Now I got to get up on the roof before it rains and tarpaper over that. They thought it was funny as hell." He paused. "One thing, though . . ."

"What's that?"

"They paid me for the drinks."

"Was anybody else in here with them?"

"Nope, nobody but me. Ever'body, they all slid out when they seen who it was."

"Did they threaten you?"

"No, they didn't. 'Course I didn' give them no cause to."

"Did you hear them say where they would go next?"

The owner shook his head. "I'm sorry. No, I didn't."

Half a dozen said the outlaws had followed the road out of town east. Reb was a day behind them; he rode to Benton, but they had not been there.

However, in Benton he met Tomas Rivera again. The scout was sitting at a table in a saloon, looking glum. He had been let go, he told Reb, because his services were no longer needed.

"The damn gover'ment's savin' money on me."

"What're you going to do?"

"Haven't figgered it out yet. Maybe go back to Texas."

Reb smiled. "I've got a proposition for you to consider."

Tomas looked at him. "What?"

"Hop Collins and his brother. Hop is worth one thousand dollars alone."

"You mean bring them in?" Tomas's eyes widened. "You know where they are?"

"No. We'd have to track them down. You're a tracker."

Tomas smiled. "How much is his brother worth?"

"Five hundred, I think."

"Where would we start lookin'?"

"In saloons. The first thing is to ask questions. Collins likes to be important. He's a big spender."

Collins and his brother were last seen in Puente. That news came over the wire and was posted in front of the weekly newspaper office. Puente was a town some forty miles east of Benton.

Reb and Tomas headed that way at once.

But when they arrived, they were told that Hop and his brother had disappeared in the night without mentioning a destination.

They were able to locate an older man who had been sitting on a bench on the main drag late and who swore he saw the Collins boys ride out toward the north. They went that way and Tomas found tracks several miles from town, not on a trail. He got down and bent low, examining the faint prints.

"Two horses," he said. "It could be them."

He was able to follow the tracks for several miles, leaning down from horseback. But when the ground changed, he got down again to look more closely. Reb swung down to walk along with him and stopped suddenly when Tomas put out his arm. "Wait—"

"What is it?"

Tomas pointed with a stubby finger. "This's the last track, right here. Never go past the last track because it could turn off in any direction. Don't move till you find the next track."

Tomas spent several minutes studying the ground from several angles, then moved slowly ahead. "They bending left a little—see this?"

"What?"

"It's a couple rabbit droppings squashed flat. This ground's hard as hell along here." He moved slowly. "Here's more of 'em . . . and some little rocks mashed into the ground." He squinted and pointed ahead. "There, the ground's softer and the track're plain. They turned left." Tomas stood and shaded his eyes. "Izzat water down there?"

Reb focused on a bit of greenery. "It's a water hole."

"Then that's why they turned." Tomas looked at the sky. "They might be camped there. Do you see any smoke?"

Reb shook his head. "No—but they're a day ahead of us. Maybe they camped there last night."

"Prob'ly did," Tomas agreed.

The tracks led directly to the distant water hole and there was ample evidence that two men had stayed a short while by the water.

But no way to know if they were the Collins boys.

Reb and Tomas camped in the same place and went on in the early morning, following plain tracks that led to a stage road running east and west. Tomas was sure the outlaws had turned west. In another day they came to Carswell, a way station manned by John Carswell. The settlement had a few shacks other than the station itself, a well, and a view of the desert.

And there was news. The stagecoach had just been robbed.

Two of the passengers had identified the robbers as the Collins brothers. One mentioned the eagle tattoo on Hop Collins's hand. They had taken a strongbox containing probably five hundred dollars in gold and some valuables. They had also frisked the passengers and grabbed watches and money. Travelers carried money. But luckily no one had resisted, so no one had been harmed.

Reb and Tomas had come in the right direction. The six-horse stagecoach had been held up a few miles east of the way station, where the road had climbed a long hill, curving gently to the top of a ridge. The brothers had been waiting near the top where the coach was moving very slowly. They had blocked the wheels so it wouldn't roll back and ordered the driver and guard off the box. The guard had sensibly tossed his weapon into the brush on order, when faced with two shotguns. The passengers had climbed out and lined up to be robbed. It had all gone very smoothly.

"They was in a good mood," one of the passengers said. "So they didn't shoot nobody."

Reaching Carswell near dark, Reb and Tomas stayed the night and investigated the hill in the morning. Tomas quickly found where the brothers had moved off into the desert. In the brush they had shot the lock off the strongbox and left it empty.

On the flats Tomas shaded his eyes. "I think they're heading for Sparrowhawk. I been there a thousand times. It's a town fulla saloons and girls. Lots of girls."

"Then that's where they'd go," Reb agreed. "Sure as a gun."

21

Sparrowhawk was a large town. It straggled along the river of the same name, on both sides, though there was only one bridge. Most of the town was on the north side where the business district was.

The bridge was very stout and wide. It had been built by railroad engineers years before, but the contemplated spur line had never come to pass. The rails had ended miles to the east at Acton. And the cattle that had once been driven to Sparrowhawk now went to Acton.

However, the town was situated on flat land and was easy to reach from all directions—and Acton was not. So people came to Sparrowhawk to trade and spend money on Bonner Street, known as the Barbary Coast of the plains.

The Collins boys had been there many times, always after a good haul, and so were generous with their victims' money. It ensured them many friends, hangers-on, and good times.

The men who owned and operated the "big three" saloon gambling casinos paid off the local law to mind its own business and stay the hell off Bonner Street . . . which it did. The three had a six-man private force to keep the peace and keep the shooting to a minimum, but also to bury the bodies when that was not possible.

The system worked to everyone's satisfaction.

The Collins brothers could feel secure there, as long as

they stayed within that one small district. If they stepped outside it, they were fair game.

Hop and Ames were especially friendly with one of the big three operators, Bart Pollak. He had grubstaked them many years before, when they were starting out; they had come to him with a plan for holding up a payroll wagon. Bart had counted out the money and the brothers had been successful and paid him back with interest.

Now, whenever they were in the vicinity, they spent their money in the Dreamland Palace, a big, noisy saloon, dance hall, and gambling casino that never closed.

But this time when they rode into town and got down in front of the Palace, they learned that Bart was away and not expected back for a week. The saloon manager, Harry Logan, greeted them expansively and bought them a drink. "Glad to see you. You all staying for a while?"

"Till Bart gets back at least," Hop said. "Thought we'd rest up."

"And get us a bath and some new duds," Ames replied, admiring Harry's crisp white shirt, cravat with the diamond stickpin, and broadcloth store suit. His boots were shined to a high gloss.

He did not look down his nose at their bedraggled condition and insisted on putting them into a room on the second floor. "Bart would want you to have the best, gents. There's a bath house downstairs. You tell the man I said it was free to you. And there's plenty of stores in town. Anything else I can get you, just ask."

"Thanks, Harry."

They spent the afternoon in the bath house, soaking and scrubbing, then went to the nearest clothing emporium outside Bonner Street, bought new clothes, and tossed away the old. After that, they visited a barbershop for shaves and haircuts, including nice-smelling lotions, liberally sprinkled on.

When they swaggered back to the Palace, Harry hardly knew them.

"You all are a sight for red eyes." They stood at the bar and Harry passed out cigars, noticing that both brothers were eyeing the girls who were circulating. These two had probably been in the tall brush for too long. Harry got them seated at a table and leaned in close.

"Wait till the other girls come downstairs, boys. You ain't got a proper selection here."

Ames pointed with his hat brim. "That dark'un there, she looks pretty good to me."

"Ah, she's just a wheeligo girl. You all sit tight for a little bit and you won't be disappointed. You lissen to Uncle Harry."

"He'll hold it," Hop said, grinning. Ames poured another drink.

Tomas was right. The tracks led straight to Sparrowhawk. They rode through the main drag and went on to Bonner Street—the "district." If the Collins boys were here, they'd be on Bonner Street. There was no sense looking anywhere else.

"What's our plan?" Tomas asked, gazing at the bright lanterns hung along the wooden awnings.

"You're no part of this," Reb said. "You got me here, but I don't want you getting dead."

"I don't want that either. But if I don't help, I can't collect any of the reward."

"You're a married man. You've got a family."

Tomas made a face. "That's why I need some of the reward money."

Reb sighed. "All right. You're in."

"Fine. What's the first thing we do?"

"Find the Collins boys. But we've got to be careful. I'm positive they've got friends here, so it won't do to ask the wrong questions."

"It might take us a month to find them just by looking at people."

Reb shook his head. "It won't take that long. I'd say there's only three places they could be. And we've got one edge.

None of the folks here know us.'' He indicated the three saloon dance halls.

Tomas said softly, ''And when we find them . . . ?''

''Then we decide what to do—based on the situation.''

''We probably won't be able to take them out of a saloon.''

Reb nodded. ''True. But they can't stay in the saloon all the time, can they?''

Tomas frowned. ''There's whiskey and girls inside. Why not?''

Harry knew what he was talking about, Ames realized when he saw the first of the new girls come downstairs. They were certainly the cream of the crop. The other girls disappeared and a three-piece band began to play: piano, violin, and mandolin. Men led some of the girls onto the floor to stomp and gyrate with others yelling and clapping hands.

Hop was sitting in on a game with three others, so Ames moved slowly through the crowded room, looking at the girls. He hadn't had a woman since Washington crossed the Delaware—or so it seemed.

Then his glances settled on one. She was dark and shapely, not too tall, and wore white ruffles on a low-cut red dress that had a pert little bustle in the back. She was dancing with an awkward young man who looked to be just off a farm. He was grinning all over a flushed face that turned pale when Ames pushed in between him and the girl and took her hand, pulling her to him.

She didn't appear at all startled, looking at him with round eyes; she did not protest, as if this happened to her constantly. The farmer said, ''Hey—watchoo doing?''

Ames gave him a look and pushed him away. The other scowled, obviously trying to make up his mind what to do, and finally gave it up and turned away. Ames paid him no more attention.

He said to the girl, ''What's your name?''

''Klara. What's yours?''

"Ames." He moved to the music with her. "I ain't much for dancin'. Let's go someplace else."

"You in a big hurry?"

He grinned at her. "I just got into town. I been out on the grass for a spell and I got money to spend."

"That makes a big difference," she said, suddenly interested. "Let's go."

She led him past the musicians on their stand, through a door, and up narrow stairs to the second floor, then toward the front. She opened a door, number six, and they went in. Ames paused to slide the bolt closed.

He was in a plain square room with small ruffles on the windows and wallpaper with tiny red stripes. The bed took up most of the space, only a sheet over a mattress. There was a small table with a lamp and one chair with a tapestried bottom.

Klara gave him a coquettish smile. "How much d'you want to spend?"

He laughed, watching her eyes. "Fifty dollars . . ."

He was not disappointed. Her eyes widened for a second and she took a sudden breath. He knew no one had ever given her that much.

Then she smiled again differently, watching him pull the bills from a pouch on his belt. He laid the money out on the chair and she scooped it up quickly.

He sat and began to remove his boots, so he couldn't see what she did with the greenbacks. She went into a closet and returned, sliding the dress off over her head. When he crawled onto the bed with her, she said, "You don't smell like a mule."

"I did a few hours ago. But I knew I was going to find you."

She chuckled, reaching for him. "Of course you did." She squeezed him. "What's my name?"

He hesitated. "Kate?"

"No."

'Oh yes, now I remember. Klara." He pushed as she guided him. "How long have you worked here?"

"It seems like forever. Three years. But it's better than a crib in an alley."

"You don't have to do this, do you? Are you looking for a husband?"

She snickered. "Of course. But I like this. And I'd like a husband—depending."

"You wouldn't marry me, though. . . ."

She shook her head. "I don't think so. You're an owlhoot, aren't you? One day you'd turn up dead."

Ames sighed. "Don't kill me off too soon."

"I've seen it happen."

"Well, what do you expect to find on Bonner Street?"

Klara rubbed his back. "No one. But when I've saved enough, I'll go back to civilization and become a church member."

"Ah. You have plans. . . ."

She slapped his bare butt. "A girl has to make plans, and sometimes they pan out. Are you one of the Collins brothers?"

"What makes you think so?"

"I saw posters in Sparrowhawk and you fit the description. You've got a brother—I forget his name—"

"His name is Hop. It's a nickname. His real name is Hobart and of course he hates it."

"You *are* notorious."

"So you'd become a church member?"

"Yes, and maybe even sing in the choir."

He laughed. "Maybe God won't notice you there."

She pinched him. "Maybe not if I keep my clothes on."

Reb and Tomas split up and moved through all three saloon dance halls looking for the Collins boys. It took awhile, but Reb found Hop at last, in a poker game. He went after Tomas and they sat on opposite sides of the room keeping Hop in view. They did not see Ames.

When the game broke up late in the evening, Hop sat and talked with several others for an hour, then wandered back past the little stage and through the door.

By the time Reb got there, Hop had disappeared. He might have gone upstairs or out the back.

There were no hotels on Bonner Street. They got a room in Sparrowhawk with two beds. It was a good bet, Reb thought, that the brothers had been put up in an upstairs saloon room.

And as long as they stayed there, it did not look as if he and Tomas would get a chance to grab them.

Tomas said, "They're not going to spend the rest of their lives on Bonner Street. We'll just have to wait 'em out."

Reb sighed inwardly. That might be true, but what if the brothers stayed a year?

Klara was seeing Simon Greene regularly. He was her man. Her bedmates were customers. Just that, transient lovers who meant nothing to her. Sometimes she hardly looked at their faces and would not have known them the next day, had they met.

Simon worked as a bartender in the Dreamland Palace bar. They planned to go east as soon as they had enough money saved.

After Ames had visited her the first time, she told Simon about him. "He's got a moneybelt stuffed full of greenbacks."

"You saw it?"

"Yeah, when he paid me. Fifty dollars!" She showed him the bills.

"Christ! Fifty dollars for a roll in the hay?"

"He's got so much fifty is nothing to him. And I bet you his brother's got the same amount. They're owlhoots, the two of them."

He nodded. "I seen Hop in the saloon. He's a friend of Bart's." He patted her cheek. "What you got in mind, honey?"

"Money." She smiled. "He shouldn't ought to have so much money and us poor."

"I 'gree with you, but he's a damn dangerous hombre. He's a gunman. You got any ideas how to get that money?"

"Yeah, I have." She bit his ear. "Lissen. . . ."

22

Reb sat in the Palace Saloon with a deck of cards and a beer at his elbow, and in a while a girl came and sat by him with a practiced smile. "Hello there . . . My name's Tessie."

Reb grinned at her. "I'm Fred."

She rubbed her knee against his. "You want some fun, Freddie?"

He looked at her innocently. "You mean like pitching horseshoes?"

She blinked, then laughed. "You're a josher, ain't you?"

"Maybe you mean cards?"

"Hell no. I mean go upstairs with me."

"What's upstairs?"

She leaned close so he smelled the cheap perfume. "Rooms with beds, honey."

"Ooooo, I see." He lowered his voice. "This's a big place. What else is upstairs?"

"Bart's rooms and the offices. I dunno, though, I never been on the other side. It's locked off from us girls."

"No one's allowed there, huh?"

"Not unless the boss says so. Why d'you care?"

He smiled. "Just curious. Wonderin' how the rich folks live."

"Yeah, me too." She rubbed his knee harder. "You comin' or not?"

"I'll pass this time, Tessie."

She shrugged and got up.

* * *

Simon was with her when she woke up. He sat in bed and reached for his Blackwell's to roll a smoke. "Your plan only gets us Ames's money. What about Hop?"

"I don't know about him. I haven't had no truck with him." Klara rubbed against him and he gave her a puff on the cigarette. She said, "But half is better'n nothing, ain't it?"

"Yeah, it is. But can you carry it off? We do it and they going to question you—maybe me too. And you waver, they might start beatin' it out of you."

"They won't find no money in my room. Why won't they believe me?"

"They'll say you got the best chance."

"I'll tell 'em nothing."

"That's my girl. Tell 'em nothing."

"When d'you want to do it?"

He frowned. "This is Tuesday. Tomorrow I'll borrow a light wagon and put it in the alley late. I go off shift at six, so there's plenty of time. Can you get him upstairs in your room for sure?"

"I think so. . . . Why the wagon?"

He looked at her curiously. "For the body. We can't leave it in your room."

"Oh—yeah. Of course not." She hadn't thought it through—or hadn't wanted to. Of course he had to die. It wasn't just a holdup. And Sime had to get rid of the body.

They agreed on the signal she would give when Ames arrived and Simon left her to go to work in the bar.

It was a long day and a nervous one; she kept thinking of the money they'd have and it eased her somewhat. Unless they played into horrendous bad luck, it should all go very smoothly.

It proved to be no trick to get Ames up to her room. He was eager for more of her charms. He bolted the door as before, but while he was grunting over his boots, removing them, she slid the bolt back, then casually arranged the window curtain in the signal. Klara had lived for two years in

St. Louis and kept up a chatter about the town as he slid into bed naked. She was suddenly playful and wanted to wrestle and it took him a few minutes to muscle her flat on her back, laughing.

She had turned the lamp low and it cast huge shadows on the opposite wall as they rolled from side to side—then he was atop her and she went limp in his arms as he made the bed groan and shake.

He never heard the man who crept into the room and who hit him powerfully across the back of the neck. She heard the crack as his spine broke, and she shuddered. Simon pulled the body off her and she slithered away from it, grabbing at her clothes.

"Is he dead?"

"Dead as a dried catfish. Lock the door."

Simon had brought an old blanket and a rope. He removed the moneybelt and slung it about his own waist, grinning at her as he felt the heft of it. Then he rolled the body in the blanket, tied the rope about it, and opened the alley window.

He was so efficient, it occurred to her to wonder if he'd ever done this before. But she did not ask him.

Looking out carefully, he could see no one in the dark alley. This was the tricky part, he whispered. He powered the body up over the sill and gritted his teeth, lowering it to the ground. That done, he tied the rope to one of the bed legs and climbed down himself as silently as possible.

Klara untied the rope and tossed it down, then closed the window.

She looked carefully at the bed sheet for bloodstains and found none. There was no blood and no evidence of a struggle. She got a bottle out of a drawer and took a deep swallow. It burned her throat; she sat on the edge of the bed and closed her eyes, waiting till her heart stopped pounding. It took awhile.

Then she smoothed the bed, got dressed, and went downstairs.

* * *

Simon dumped the body in the light wagon and drove out of town by back streets. Several miles out he pulled the bundle out and rolled it down an incline into the weeds.

He made a cigarette, turned the wagon around, and returned. A good night's work. Very profitable. He was eager to count the money, but that would have to wait for the removal of all suspicion.

Klara was very likely to be suspected—and they would also suspect him because many knew about him and Klara. They'd never made a secret of it. He was living in a boardinghouse not far from the saloon. He dropped off the borrowed wagon and walked home, taking the alley that led to the house stable. A long time before, he had built a hiding place in the stable wall where he kept his and Klara's saved money. Banks were so untrustworthy. He slid the heavy moneybelt into the narrow space and closed it off. It would take a half-dozen men a week to find it—if indeed they found it at all.

Then he went to bed.

Simon was mildly surprised the next day, when he showed up for work, that there was no outcry about Ames Collins.

He did his work, and when Klara came downstairs later, she gave him a tiny little shrug as if to say nothing was happening. That was all to the good. The longer it took for anyone to find the body, the better.

He got a chance for a few words with her across the bar. "Don't even mention his name to anyone. You've forgot it."

"Don't worry."

The big noise came later, another day later, when someone stumbled over the body and brought it into town.

Hop Collins was mad as hell! Some son of a bitch had killed and robbed Ames! And worse, there were no clues at all. One of Bart's policemen said he was positive the man had been killed somewhere else and dumped there.

Who had seen him last?

A lot of names were mentioned, and finally they got around to girls. Hadn't Ames hired some of the girls? Hop asked the bartenders, but none of them knew. Until he offered a hundred dollars for information.

Then a note was slipped under his door. A man offered to meet him and tell him what he knew. Hop met the man in the place suggested and learned that Ames had been seen at least once with a saloon girl, Klara.

And Klara was cozy with a barman who worked the day shift at the Palace, Simon Greene.

Hop paid the man and went to talk to Bart, who had returned. Bart was a bear of a man, with huge hands and rumpled clothes. He was never seen without a cigar. He listened to Hop and sent two men to search Klara's room.

They turned up nothing of interest.

Bart had the girl brought to his office. "When did you see Ames Collins last?"

She was scared, with all the men staring and frowning at her. "Jeez, Mr. Bart, I dunno . . . a day or two ago, I guess." She had an inspiration. "Did he complain about me?"

"No. You don't remember exactly?"

Klara shook her head. "There's quite a few, sir. It's hard to remember. . . ."

Bart stared at her a moment. "All right. Go back to your room and stay there."

He sent a man to sit in front of her door for an hour. Two others went to search Simon Greene's room at the boarding-house.

They turned up nothing.

Bart said to Hop, "Looks like they had nothing to do with it. I figger somebody saw him winning at the tables and followed him outside. It happens."

Hop sighed deeply. "Then we'll never catch 'im."

"No. Prob'ly not. Too bad, Hop. But we'll give him a damn good send-off."

The funeral was held the next afternoon in the cemetery

outside the town on a gentle hill. A dozen people turned out in a light rain to hear the preacher and watch the stained pine box lowered into the freshly dug grave.

Klara did not attend. Neither did Simon.

23

The news of Ames Collins's murder was all over town in no time. Reb and Tomas discussed it, sitting in tilted-back chairs in front of the General Bisbee Saloon.

Tomas said, "Somebody killed him for the money he carried."

"How would anyone know he carried money? Wouldn't he be careful not to show it?"

"I'd think so, but maybe he told someone . . . someone he thought he could trust. Someone got close enough to kill him."

Reb mused. "He probably had a moneybelt of some kind." He scratched his chin and looked at the other. "And he probably wore it under his shirt. But he'd undress in front of a whore girl, wouldn't he? She'd see it, huh?"

Tomas nodded. "He'd undress at the bath house, too."

"But less chance of anyone seeing the moneybelt there."

"Umm, I suppose so."

"So how are we going to find out which whore girl he was visiting? Maybe he saw half a dozen."

"And whores aren't noted for telling the truth."

"I've heard that," Reb said. "We could concentrate on the one who leaves town."

Tomas regarded him curiously. "You think a girl killed him and took the body out of town?"

"No. She'd have to have help, unless she was one hell of a big powerful female."

"And if so, she'd wait for a few months before leaving town for good, wouldn't she? Otherwise it'd be suspicious."

Reb said, "And there's one other thing. . . ."

"What's that?"

"If someone killed Ames for his money, will they make a try for Hop? He must have as much as his brother had."

"Ummm," Tomas said. "I didn't think of that."

"Yeah, maybe we ought to be watching Hop."

His brother's death affected Hop more than he liked. It meant he was alone, no other kin in the world. And now there was no one he could really trust.

He sat alone in the Palace bar, his back to the wall, the night of the funeral. It wasn't easy to accept that Ames was gone; they'd been together so many, many years.

Hop stared at the men in the noisy room. How would he go about finding someone to take Ames's place? They'd had their little differences from time to time, but never anything serious.

And Ames had been a very experienced and watchful man, trained by a rough and unrelenting life. How had someone managed to club him to death? He had eyes in the back of his head and ears like an Indian. How had it been possible? When he was asleep? That seemed the most likely. The doc had said one single hard blow had been struck on the back of Ames's neck, snapping it.

Hop did not doubt Ames had been killed for the money he carried. Did that mean *he* might be the next target? Hop rubbed the walnut grip of his pistol. It was a possibility. He had even more money than Ames because he'd been winning at poker. Ames had never been much of a gambler.

He watched the crowd. It was no different than any other crowd in any other town . . . maybe a few more hard cases among the pilgrims because it was Bonner Street. He owed nothing to anyone here, not even to Bart.

What if he slid out nice and easy one night soon and went south?

He could go down into Texas, as far as Santone; he knew

people there. Maybe he could pick up a partner. He would like to stay and find Ames's killer, but that might prove impossible. There was no connection between them, killer and victim, but the money. And that was easy to conceal. He could spend his life looking . . . and find nothing.

So why not go? The more he thought about it, the better it sounded. Slide out easy, say nothing to anyone, not even to Bart. He could always drop Bart a line later and explain.

There was one necessity, food for the journey—at least part of it. He would stay away from towns, maybe until he got to Texas. So it was necessary to go into Sparrowhawk to a general store; there were none on Bonner Street.

Reb and Tomas tailed him there. Tomas even went inside the store while Hop was buying vittles, and put airtights into a grain sack, never once looking at Hop. He was just another customer.

They watched Collins tie on the food sack and head south out of town, avoiding Bonner Street.

Tomas said to Reb, "He bought enough to last him a week. He's going somewhere in a serious hurry. I'd guess Oklahoma."

"As good a guess as any . . ."

They followed, but had to stay miles back in the flat country. Reb used his binoculars constantly, wary of an ambush. At night they moved closer, but Hop always camped off the trail, and when Tomas attempted to crawl close the first night, Hop fired at him. The shot went wild, but it proved Hop was alert.

Tomas said, "He heard something and got a shot off. But he doesn't know what he fired at and he'll think it was a small animal—unless he moves."

But he did not. Morning proved he was still there. He made a small fire and an hour later got on his horse and went south again.

It was a cool day with lowering clouds. Collins set a fast pace that morning as if he were in a hurry. They followed,

but much slower because they came to ambush spots that had
to be circled. But each time they did, they found no evidence
that Hop had hesitated. Apparently he did not suspect that
he was tailed.

Tomas said, "I'm sure he thinks he's alone. He's easily
two or three hours ahead of us now and moving steadily."

"Could we lose him?"

"We might—if it rains hard enough to wash out the tracks.
So far they're plain enough."

They were very plain for two days.

Then they came to a dry lake bed. It was pale and
hard and swept clean by winds and their horses' hooves
left no mark. Neither had Hop's. Tomas could find not one
single track. Hop Collins had gone directly into the lake
bed.

"We can only hope," Tomas said, "that he went straight
across, so we can pick him up on the other side."

But he had not. Somewhere on the lake bed he had turned
off, but which way?

It took a full day to discover where he had left the lake—
far to the east—then swung south again.

"He did it to lose any pursuit," Tomas said definitely. "It
doesn't mean he knows we're after him. He's an owlhoot; it's
just second nature. He's devious."

On the far side of the lake they came into low hills, and
as they reached them mottled clouds moved in and a light
drizzle began to fall. Tomas swore, growling that the tracks
would be gone if it got heavier.

When they came to Kettown, it was long after dark; they
had seen the lights from a distance. It was a way station on
the stage road, a small collection of shacks around a fieldstone building housing the station itself. Behind the station
were corrals and sheds and a large barn.

The owner, Tucker Ket, had no room for them; they were
all occupied, but he let them sleep in the barn.

He had not seen a traveler of Hop Collins's description.

The station had a small grub shop run by the owner's wife,
where they had breakfast. In the morning they set out along

the road to find where Hop had crossed it. They rode several miles to the west and found nothing. Reb thought their chances were very slim.

Tomas, however, was sure they'd find hoofprints—and he was proved right. Hop Collins had crossed the road a half mile east of the station, heading south.

Tomas got down and examined the tracks closely. "It's his horse," he said. "The left front shoe is a 'good enough.' I'd know it in my sleep."

They followed the tracks the rest of the day, winding out of the hills, across a wide stretch of prairie land, and through stands of blackjack oaks. Many times they lost the trail, but picked it up again farther on. Hop was making no attempt to hide his tracks. Obviously he had no idea he was being tailed. Tomas estimated he was at least a day ahead of them.

Then the weather began to change and a storm appeared out of the northwest. For a time the wind blew hard, then raindrops spattered down and they took shelter under a group of oaks and watched the trickles of water become streams.

"There goes the trail," Tomas said sadly. "There won't be a thing left of it tomorrow."

"There's only one thing to do, go on south. Do you suppose we're in Oklahoma yet?"

"Either that or we're close."

It took half a day more to wait out the rain. When it let up, they continued south in a mist and at dusk halted on a rise and saw the lights of Cameron in the distance. They came into the town two hours later with Tomas sniffling.

The hotel provided a bath house and he sat in the steam for a long while. Reb talked to several bartenders, who told him a man of Hop's description had been in the bar two days ago. Collins had also stayed in the hotel, giving his name as John Colyer.

In the morning Tomas had a full-blown cold, with stuffy head and a cough. He felt poorly, eyes watering and bones sore. He was prone to such, he said, and feared it would turn into pneumonia. Reb bought him a bottle of whiskey and learned in the store that the nearest doctor was forty miles away. But Tomas did not feel like traveling. He wanted to stay in bed a week, he said, with the bottle. He had great faith in whiskey to cure whatever ailed him.

They were just over the line into Oklahoma. Reb bought supplies, promised Tomas he would return, and did not linger in the town. There was a trail leading south and he took it to Dakins, a wide place with only three shacks. But an old-timer swore a man of Hop's description had been there a day and a half ago.

After Dakins the trail approached a line of sand hills and veered west sharply. Reb left the trail and camped that night in a small woods by a quick-flowing brown creek. Hop Collins had given him the slip a long while ago—had he done it again? He might know this country very well.

The next morning he spent several hours looking for tracks and found none he thought might be Collins's. Tomas had pointed out the slight peculiarities of the left front horseshoe, to no avail.

Where had Collins gone? He had been pointing south for days. Had he reached his destination? Had he turned off? Or was he still moving south?

It was easy to feel discouraged, but Reb went on doggedly and in late afternoon came onto a well-rutted road that ran vaguely southeast. He stepped down and walked along the road, looking for the tracks of a single horse, and was unsuccessful. Neither could he find where a horseman had crossed the road. And when the sun was low in the west, he gave it up.

He followed the road into the town of Berriman, arriving very late and very tired. He got a room in the hotel and barely got his boots off before he fell across the bed and went to sleep.

In the morning he had breakfast in a restaurant and contemplated his future over a plate of eggs. Probably Hop Collins was long gone. He had to face the fact that he would probably never collect the bounty on the owlhoot. He had invested much time on the Collins brothers, lost one to an intruder, and now had lost the other to the winter rains. It was very discouraging.

24

Reb visited the local deputy sheriff, Henry Alford, and looked over his sheaf of wanted dodgers. Alford was a young, affable man who had been on the job only a year. He pulled out one sheet, laid it on his desk, and rapped it with a knuckle.

"This one is giving everyone a lot of trouble. He's a stage robber and nobody seems able to catch him."

Reb read the particulars. The robber was called El Lobo by the newspapers, real name unknown. His first appearance in the territory had been a year and a half ago when he had robbed a stage not far from Berriman.

Subsequently he had killed one guard and three passengers. The guard had been slow in complying with his order to toss down the gun. The passengers had tried to hide valuables.

He was apt to show up anyplace and anytime, but occasionally a month or more apart. The bounty on him was eleven hundred dollars. A sizable amount. There was no known picture of him except an artist's sketch, which was almost useless since it showed only a heavy-shouldered man wearing a mask, dark clothes, and a hat.

Reb asked, "When was his last robbery?"

"About a month ago on the road to Corona. Before that he robbed a stage on the Riverton road and before that on the same Corona road but in a different place, just outside of town. All the robberies have been within about a sixty-mile circle."

"So he's got it in for this stage company. . . . What's your theory?"

The deputy shrugged lightly. "I think he's building a nest egg for his old age."

"Does he seem to know when there's a strongbox on the stage?"

"No—at least that's my opinion. He's stolen some strong-boxes, but missed others."

"That's interesting. How old d'you think he is?"

"I've asked some of the passengers who had a good look at him and they all say the same thing. He's in his forties."

Reb went outside and sat in a chair on the walk and thought about it. El Lobo hit the stages at random, so he probably worked alone. He was apparently content to take what he could, not at all like Hop Collins, who would probably have had someone in the stage office to let him know when a good haul was being shipped.

But if he met the bandit at work, it would only be by chance. And he might easily ride back and forth for a year and never see him. But what else could he do? Eleven hundred dollars was a lot of money. It would take him more than a year to earn that much as a cowhand. So it was worth taking a whack at bringing El Lobo to justice.

He had another talk with the deputy, telling him he had decided to find the bandit if he could. The deputy said most of the holdups had taken place in the forenoon. El Lobo's weapon was a double-barreled shotgun and he always met the stage on a hill or a curve where the stage was slowed. He rode a black horse and usually threatened to shoot one of the stage horses so the driver pulled up.

Black horses were not common and it was generally held that El Lobo wanted to be recognized instantly; his hat and clothes were black also. It was part of his threat. In the past he had not hesitated to kill when his commands were not quickly obeyed.

The deputy had long ago put out inquiries about black horses; but they had led to nothing. "I think he's got a hide-out somewhere in that sixty-mile circle. His clothes and horse are like a costume. He prob'ly comes into town dressed like ever'one else, riding an ordinary brown nag.''

Reb agreed. It was a very good theory. He bought a shotgun and spent a week riding the stages back and forth. But El Lobo did not appear.

It gave him time to ruminate on his calling . . . which was that of a bounty hunter. He had to be successful in order to carry on, to support himself while he looked for and brought in his next fugitive.

But of course it had one great advantage. He worked for himself and took orders from no one. That one thing made all the difference.

He rode the stagecoach to Riverton again, and when he returned, the Corona stage driver had brought news. El Lobo had not only been seen near Corona, but had been fired upon by several hunters. One of them was certain he had hit the bandit, who had galloped off.

They had found bloodstains on some brush.

Reb went to Corona at once and talked to the hunter, a middle-aged merchant. He, with two others from the town, had been hunting deer north of the town in the foothills.

''We left our horses and walked up a draw,'' the man said, ''figgering to spread out. We were sitting down, taking a rest, when this rider come along a ridge in front of us. He was ridin' a black horse, had on black clothes, and we all said, 'Jesus! It's El Lobo!' ''

''What'd you do then?''

''Well, we all jumped up and yelled and the hombre heard us a-course and pulled a pistol.''

''He fired at you?''

''Yeah. The shot went over our heads and he spurred his horse. I had a good shot at him and I think I put two bullets in him. When we climbed out of the draw, we found bloodstains. I hit 'im all right!''

''What'd you do then?''

''We went back and got our horses, which took awhile. We tried to follow him, but we lost the trail pretty quick.''

''How bad hurt d'you think he was?''

"Hard to tell, but there was a lot of blood."

Reb unfolded a map. "Show me where you saw him."

The deputy got on the telegraph notifying all the doctors in the vicinity of the possibility that El Lobo would come in for treatment.

Reb took the stage for Corona.

He got a horse at the livery and visited the town doctor at once. El Lobo had not approached him—nor had anyone else with a gunshot wound.

Reb then rode into the foothills, following the map. He searched the area all day and all the next day, finding nothing. The third day he went farther eastward and came onto a tiny meadow where a black horse was cropping grass.

Circling the meadow, the shotgun ready, Reb found no one near. The black horse was saddled, and when he approached, he saw the saddle covered with crusted blood that had run down to one stirrup. El Lobo had indeed been hit bad.

But he could not locate a body. He took the horse in finally and went back the next day with Deputy Alford. They scoured the foothills and wooded area with no result.

"He's found a hiding place," Alford said, "and crawled in and died. One day we'll find his bones."

"And quite a lot of money," Reb said.

"Yeah, more than likely."

As they rode back the deputy left him in sight of the town, saying he had promised to see someone about a missing mule team. Reb took the stage road into town; it had been misty all morning and part of the day. The tracks of a horse pulling a light wagon were very sharp and clear on the damp roadway—and so were the tracks of a single horse.

Reb swung down and examined them closely. One hoofprint was particularly defined, made by a horse with one "good enough" shoe. Hop Collins!

Collins had gone into Corona only hours before!

The tracks mingled with others on the main street. Reb

went at once to the bank and talked to the manager, saying Hop Collins was in town. The flustered manager quickly alerted his people and Reb went to the hotel, where he learned a pilgrim had registered as John Conners that morning.

"He's growin' a beard," the clerk told him. "Perty surly feller."

"Is he in his room?"

"No. He went out awhile ago."

Reb visited the two restaurants, then began with the saloons. Several of the larger had closed card rooms and girls' cubicles upstairs. He could not search them all without raising a ruckus.

Another clerk was on duty when he returned to the hotel. No, he had not seen John Conners, the clerk said—didn't know what he looked like. His key was not on the nail, so he might be in his room or the key might be in his pocket.

Reb sat in a chair on the walk till dark and Collins had not appeared. Possibly he had come to town to see someone.

Over coffee in the restaurant across the street, he thought about home, wondering if his father had remarried. Rustin was only about a hundred miles north; he could be there in a few days.

Making a living as a bounty hunter was an up-and-down existence. How many times had Hop Collins given him the slip? That was what he was going to have to put up with if he remained his own boss. He would spend endless hours chasing down a man like El Lobo, and in the end it would all come to naught.

But he *was* his own boss. It was what he'd always wanted. And it was worth it if now and then he collected. He had spent days and days hunting Hop Collins, for instance, and it had never paid off. Collins was slippery as a bucket of eels.

He'd have to face it, not every chase was going to be successful.

He sighed deeply. In the morning he'd go over the deputy's stack of wanted dodgers and pick out a few possibles.

Or should he go home to Rustin first?

Sleep on it, he told himself. See how he felt in the morning. He got up, paid his bill, and walked out into the early evening.

And halted in surprise.

Coming across the street toward him was Hop Collins, obviously bound for the restaurant. But when he saw Reb halt, he also stopped, frowning. His outlaw's sixth sense was possibly telling him there was danger. . . .

In a conversational, flat voice Reb said, ''You're Hop Collins.''

And instantly Collins went for his gun.

Reb drew and fired twice. Collins's shot went into the sky. He was knocked backward to sprawl in the street, belly up. The pistol dropped from lifeless fingers.

Reb took a deep breath, staring at the downed man. The long chase was suddenly over.

People gathered to gawk, the deputy appeared, and then the undertaker's wagon hauled the body away. In his office the deputy signed the papers and Reb climbed the hotel steps to his room.

In the morning he'd start for home.

About the Author

Arthur Moore is the author of numerous Westerns. He lives in West-
lake Village, California.